W9-BZS-339

LULU

THE

BROADWAY MOUSE

TINY DREAMER. BIG DREAM.

JENNA GAVIGAN

RP | KIDS
PHILADELPHIA

• •

Running Press Kids
Hachette Book Group
1290 Avenue of the Americas, New York, NY 10104
www.runningpress.com/rpkids
@RP_Kids

Printed in the United States of America

Originally published in hardcover and ebook by Running Press Kids in October 2018. First Paperback Edition: March 2020

Published by Running Press Kids, an imprint of Perseus Books, LLC, a subsidiary of Hachette Book Group, Inc. The Running Press Kids name and logo is a trademark of the Hachette Book Group.

The Hachette Speakers Bureau provides a wide range of authors for speaking events. To find out more, go to www.hachettespeakersbureau.com or call (866) 376-6591.

The publisher is not responsible for websites (or their content) that are not owned by the publisher.

Print book cover design by Frances J. Soo Ping Chow.
Print book interior design by T. L. Bonaddio and Frances J. Soo Ping Chow.

Library of Congress Control Number: 2019938860

ISBNs: 978-0-7624-6459-3 (paperback), 978-0-7624-6461-6 (hardcover), 978-0-7624-6460-9 (ebook)

LSC-C

10 9 8 7 6 5 4 3 2 1

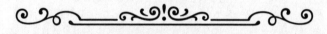

FOR JAYNE AND JIM GAVIGAN, WHO DID IT ALL FOR
THEIR TINY DAUGHTER AND HER VERY BIG DREAM.

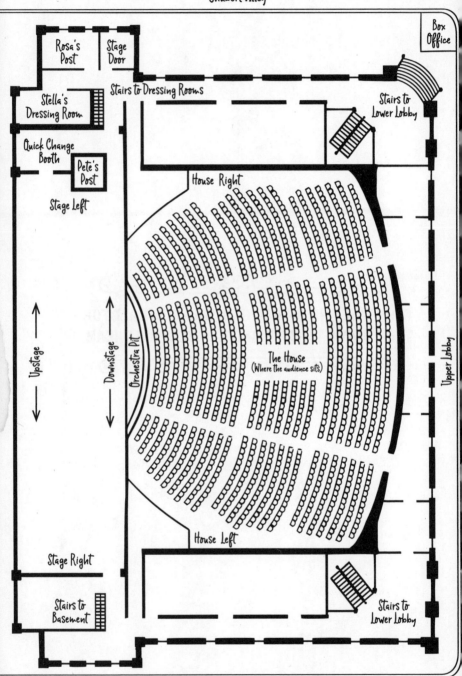

Shubert Alley

Box Office

Rosa's Post

Stage Door

Stairs to Dressing Rooms

Stella's Dressing Room

Stairs to Lower Lobby

Quick Change Booth

Pete's Post

House Right

Stage Left

Upstage

Downstage

Orchestra Pit

The House
(Where the audience sits)

Upper Lobby

Stage Right

House Left

Stairs to Basement

Stairs to Lower Lobby

Alley between Shubert and Broadhurst

HERE'S THE SCOOP

NOT TO BRAG (WELL, THIS IS MY STORY, SO I guess if I'm going to brag, this is the place to do it, right?), but my house is the most beautiful, most magical, most jaw-droppingly fabulous place in the world. (If I'm going to brag, I may as well *full-out* brag, right?)

How do I know these facts, you ask? How am I certain that my house is all these things and more? Sure, it's the only place I've ever lived. Sure, I've never been off Forty-Fourth Street, let alone the island of Manhattan. Sure, you're telling yourself that "my house is the most beautiful, most magical, most jaw-droppingly fabulous place in the world" should be categorized as an opinion, rather than a fact. A fact needs to be proven, right?

Hold on a second. This is a novel, not some scientific document. It's a story, *my* story, so if I say something's true, it's true. But to appease all you science lovers out there, I'll give you a bit of information about my house and you can come to your own conclusion—you can *deduce*. (Ugh, I sound like that know-it-all *Amanda*. More on her later . . .)

On my house's ornate, hand-painted ceiling hang four prizewinning pumpkin-sized crystal chandeliers. In my house's biggest room there are precisely one thousand four hundred forty-seven blue-green velvet seats. There are more than a dozen rooms full of makeup and wigs and costumes, and the people who inhabit these rooms are the best, most interesting, most loving people you'll ever meet. Sometimes, it's so quiet you could hear a pin drop (literally, there are hundreds of pins of different varieties all over the building), but gloriously loud at other times with the sounds of instruments and singing and (sigh) applause. I mean, really, is there anything more twitter-pating than the sound of applause?

If you've yet to guess what kind of house I live in, then this may not be the story for you. But please keep reading because some grown-up already bought the book for you, and they (and I) will be heartbroken if you don't finish it.

My house? It's a theatre. A *Broadway* theatre. (And yes, it's thea*tre* not thea*ter*. I'm not being fancy, it's just correct.)

I know what you're thinking. This narrator is bluffing. She's a liar. She's a fraud! People don't *live* in Broadway theatres. Sure, they *work* in theatres. They sew costumes, move scenery, or play the trombone. They (big sigh) perform onstage. But *people* certainly don't *live* in Broadway theatres.

Well, dear reader, you are correct. People don't. But mice, mice certainly do. *She's a mouse*, you say? Excellent powers of deduction, dear reader. 'Tis true. I'm Lulu the Mouse, and the Shubert Theatre at 225 West 44th Street in New York City? It's my house.

Now that you know my address and my name, you really only need to know one more thing about me in order to read my story.

It's the thing I daydream and nightdream about.

The thing I wish for and hope for and practice for.

The thing that makes me . . . well . . . *different* from other mice.

I want to be on Broadway. I want it more than anything in the world.

CHAPTER
ONE

L UCY LOUISE!" A BOOMING VOICE YELLS. No microphone necessary; ladies and gentlemen, meet my mother. Unlike most parents, who reserve full-name hollers for when a kid's in trouble, my mother insists on calling me by my full name at all times. It's like all these years later, she's still proud of its adorable alliterativeness (aka the back-to-back Ls). I mean, I'm not a baby anymore. Get over it, lady. You know what else is adorable and alliterative? Lulu, my nickname and stage name. Try it sometime. (P.S. I love my mom more than I love cookies, tap shoes, and Stephen Sondheim. P.P.S. Don't tell Stephen Sondheim.)

"Kinda busy, Mom," I yell back. I'm in my nest stretching: legs in a wide V, arms out in front of me so my stomach is *almost* flat on the ground. So help me, I will be able to do a center split by spring.

"I gave birth to you, young lady!" Mom shouts. See? She's obsessed. "You have twenty seconds to sit down for dinner!"

"Coming!" I practically sing as I dramatically whip around my neck like a scarf the piece of chartreuse ribbon our costumer Bet gave me, careful not to get it caught in my whiskers. I learned this signature move from Heather Huffman, one of our most glamorous cast members. She's famous for her entrances, exits, and impossibly high heels. When we first met, I looked up at her and said, "Wow, you're tall," and she replied, "Honey, it's the shoes." Since then, we've been as close to best friends as a (human) grown-up and (mouse) kid can be.

I emerge from my nest to find my dad setting our dining room table, which just happens to be a vintage dictionary, circa 1925. Scurrying around the layers of rusty pipes and old wires that line the ceiling above our dining room table are my four brothers. Yes, you read that correctly: *four brothers*. (Shout-out to any youngest siblings with a big family of mostly boys. We'll get through this together.)

If in the future I mention "the Hooligans" please know I'm referring to my big brothers, whose actual names are Walter Brooks, Matthew, Timothy, and Benjamin—Walt, Matty, Timmy, and Benji for short. (Walt is my parents' firstborn, so they named him after the Walter Kerr and Brooks Atkinson Theatres, aka my parents' childhood homes. Don't ask why they didn't just give Matthew the name Brooks, unless you want to listen to a very long story about tradition and ancestors and yada blah blah, don't ask.)

"Boys!" my mother snaps. "I sewed on so many beads today I can barely see straight. Your father went to work at five a.m. and has been cooking for the last hour. Sit. Down. Now."

The Hooligans dismount their jungle gym of pipes and wires and proceed to fight over seats—even though we've been sitting on the same matchboxes since the beginning of time—and then finally settle in.

"Nice scarf, Lulu." This is Benji. He's only a tiny bit older than I am and had trouble saying "Lucy Louise" when he was little, so I've got him to thank for my *très chic* (that's French for "very fancy"), marquee-ready nickname. I've got Walt and Matty to thank for the little hook at the end of my tail. One of them—we're still not sure which, as they're identical twins—stepped on me when I was three weeks old and the end of my tail has looked like a witch's finger ever since.

"Thanks. It's silk. Don't touch it." They're forever touching things with their (frankly) filthy feet.

My dad barely has time to get his signature Tuesday night corn soufflé on the table before my brothers are devouring it like the little beasts they are. It's a good thing I'm small and don't need much food. Honestly.

"Chew, please!" Mom says. My mother may sound like she's scolding, but in truth she's just a loud New Yorker who enjoys nothing more than "watching her loves eat."

Per usual, my dad made himself a separate soufflé sans salt; he's got an issue with salt, the issue being, he can't have any or his ears will explode. No, not *literally*. Long story short, he's got this inner ear disease and salt makes him dizzy and pukey and he'd far rather eat bland food than be sick all the time, so . . . no salt for him.

"Thank you for this beautiful meal, dear," my mother says.

"You're very welcome," my dad says.

Married forever and my parents still look at each other like they're teenagers in love. Heather Huffman says this kind of love is "more rare than the Hope Diamond." She knows *everything*.

"How was work?" my mother asks.

"Oh, fine. Fine. Nothing to report. Cold out today," Dad says.

I have zero idea what my dad does for work nor do I really care because I'm positive it has nothing to do with the theatre. My mom, on the other hand, works in the wardrobe department with Bet, our head costumer and seamstress. Yes, like the mice in *Cinderella*. We're cool with the comparisons. Those mice did a lot of good for the image of our species.

"Let's 'talk about day,'" my mother says. Apparently when he was tiny, Timmy looked up at my mom from his nest and said, "Talk about day?" in an effort to keep her from leaving. Since then "talk about day" is a dinnertime, pre-bedtime tradition in the Mouse family.

"Not much to tell," Walt says.

"This is true," Matty says, not-so-slyly winking at Walt.

"So, you weren't in the basement of the Broadhurst playing with those boys I told you not to play with?" my mother asks. "That was just a heinous rumor?"

"H-I-E-N-O-U-S," Walt recites.

"H-E-I," Timmy says with a smart smile.

"Oh, like you're such a saint," Matty says. "I saw you reading that *Frozen* program. Did it just magically fly across Forty-Fourth Street?"

"That's enough," my dad says. "Benji. How about you?"

"I helped stage management with some paperwork," Benji says. "Audience attendance is up, despite the weather." The moment they let mice produce a Broadway show, Benji will be ready.

"Lulu?" my mother asks.

"I've almost got my center split," I say. "And I think I finally mastered the tap combination for the Act Two finale."

"I'm sure you have," my mother says, in that way mothers do. "And your sewing practice?"

"I'll get to it," I say. And I will. I never lie to my mother. "It's just—"

"Rehearsing the show is more fun," my mother says.

Just then, a rumble from upstairs. A gentle vibration, a hum, a murmur. I always feel it first, before hearing it.

Activity. Something beginning. If you've ever seen the musical *West Side Story*, think of the song the lead guy, Tony, sings at the beginning about "something coming"—that's how I'm feeling right now.

I look at the clock: 6:30. All this fussing over my silk chartreuse ribbon-scarf and measly portion of corn soufflé and I almost missed it.

"Company, this is your Half-Hour call," Pete's voice booms over the intercom. "Half Hour, please, Half Hour."

"Half Hour already?" my dad says.

"You know we do Tuesdays at seven now, Dad." He knows this.

"Oh, that's right. Well, no daughter of mine can be late for her Half-Hour call. Hurry up, Lulu," Dad says. "I'll keep some soufflé warm for you in case you're hungry later."

"Thank you!" I kiss him on the cheek and scurry off faster than you can say "*Hocus Pocus* should be a Broadway musical."

"But come right down after the first number, miss!" my mom calls after me. "Get that sewing practice done before bed and then you won't have to worry about it tomorrow."

I'm running, now. Actually running. If a human walked by, they'd probably mistake me for a whirling ball of flying dust. Being late for Half Hour is a really big deal. Half Hour means that the show will begin in, well . . . a half an hour. If a cast member isn't in the building and signed in on the sign-in sheet by Half Hour, they can't perform. And while on paper I'm not an actual cast member, I sure am in my heart.

"Lucy Louise!" she shouts again.

"Yes, Mom, I heard you! Sewing before bed!" I belt.

I get to our living room door (aka the entrance to the basement level of backstage) and weave my way up the rubber-coated, nonslip stairs to the dressing rooms.

CHAPTER
TWO

M Y EYELASH, PLEASE," HEATHER HUFFMAN
instructs, holding out her hand, into which
I place her left eyelash. (Hold, please. Let
me be clear: these are false eyelashes. She buys them in
bulk at Duane Reade, preferably with a coupon. What's
that you say? *Broadway actors have to buy their own
makeup?* It's true. Bananas, right?)

Heather Huffman expertly taps on just the right
amount of eyelash glue, blows on it to dry it a bit so it's
not goopy, then applies it to her lash line. I've seen her
do this exactly three hundred and twenty-two times, but
it never gets old.

"Did I tell you I looked into getting the semi-permanent ones applied?" she asks. She has told me.

"Nope," I fib. Heather Huffman loves to talk, and I love to listen.

"Well, let's just say, I can either pay my rent or have semi-permanent eyelashes put on," H.H. says matter-of-factly. "Liner, please."

"Charcoal or brown-ish black?" These are the two she frequents the most.

"It's the first show of the week. It's snowing. Let's spice things up. Rum Raisin." I roll her the fabled liner; the last time she used it was on her birthday when she needed to be "reminded of her youth." Whatever you do, do not ask Heather Huffman her age.

H.H. looks into her magnifying mirror and cringes. "If my eyes weren't so bad, I would throw this witchy mirror right out the window. The evils it shows me. I swear I was just twenty-two." Then she looks at me and says, "Did I mention that color is heavenly on you?

Chartreuse. Tricky color, but not for you." And she really means it.

"Thanks!" I grin. "Time for stockings?"

"Indeed," H.H. says.

Our stocking routine is as follows, and please note, we've gotten it down to under twenty-five seconds, start to finish. She tosses her stockings down to the floor, then I scurry down her legs, bunch up the stockings with my feet—gently, so I don't rip them—and she easily slides her feet into them and efficiently pulls them up her legs. Try this bundling technique the next time you put on leggings or stockings. It's brilliant. Promise.

Heather Huffman has what we in show business call "legs for days," which basically means her legs are much longer and leaner than most, perfect for dancing, posing, and making an entrance, be it onstage or at the diner. She made her Broadway debut at age eighteen, in a show called *La Cage aux Folles*, in which she played a boy who dressed like a girl. She's been working steadily ever since. She's very proud of the fact that she's never had a job outside of show business. "Steady employment in show business is not the norm, Lulu. They should tell them that at theatre school graduation. Or better yet, at application. Ha! I love it when I rhyme unintentionally."

Post-stocking routine, H.H. begins to "prep" her hair, which is something every performer has to do before his or her wig goes on. (Some choose to do it themselves; some have our hair supervisor Jeremiah or another member of the hair staff do it for them.) H.H. sits in front of her mirror, picks up a section of her honey-colored hair—there will be a dozen or so sections by the time this process is over—and begins to wind it around her finger, pinning the curl tightly in place at her scalp with two bobby pins. As she moves on to pin curl number two we hear: "I'm here, I'm here. Don't panic. I'm here."

In whirls Jodie Howard, her show wig already on and four tote bags falling off of her snow-coated shoulders. I have never seen Jodie Howard without at least one tote bag on each shoulder. In her own words, she "lugs her life around in them." Need anything—aspirin, dental floss, a Lipton tea bag—she's your gal.

"You're late," Heather Huffman says, calmly pinning down a third curl. If I had to compare the ladies to weather, Heather Huffman would be a rainstorm. She's steady and much welcomed most of the time, with an occasional burst of thunder and lightning. But Jodie Howard? I say this with love: she's a tornado.

"I practically hurled myself into the theatre at six thirty-one," Jodie says, loudly. "Pete looked the other way, the saint. I went straight into hair." She may be a tornado but she's also hands down one of the funniest people I've ever met. She's loud, she's sassy; she's a self-described "hoot." She's Scuttle from *The Little Mermaid*, if Scuttle were a middle-aged blonde woman from Long Island.

Jodie and H.H. share a dressing room. Neither of them was happy about it at first—both claimed they had reached a level in their careers that warranted private dressing rooms—but they love each other now. After their first week in the theatre during Tech, once they'd gotten to know each other a bit more (thanks to a week of back-to-back twelve-hour days), Heather Huffman admitted she'd been a bit jealous of Jodie, which was why she'd fought the roommate situation.

"A regular person's ego is a powerful thing, Tiny." H.H. calls me Tiny because, well, I'm tiny.

"An actress's ego is a powerful *monster*." She felt it was important for me—"as a female"—to understand the difference between jealousy and envy. See? She knows *everything*.

"Envy," she told me, midsip of her nonfat latte, "envy is when you want what someone else has. I'm envious of my sister's emerald-cut engagement ring, for example."

"I feel ya," I said. "It's so sparkly." She and her sister go to lunch between shows every Saturday so I've met her—and the ring—dozens of times.

"Jealousy is when you're worried someone is trying to take what you have." She explained she was jealous of Jodie, of her ability to be the center of attention. H.H. had always been the center of attention, and she wasn't ready to give it up.

"But then I realized there's plenty of attention to go around. She makes 'em laugh, and I, well . . ." She winked. "I make 'em swoon. We're better together, you know? A team."

They're planning a revival of the musical *Mame* for when they're "much older." No word yet on who will play Auntie Mame and who will play Vera. I'm guessing they'll compete in some sort of friendly duel involving comedic timing, fur coats, and lung capacity.

Back in the right now, Jodie is doing a series of lunges, an "integral" part of her preshow routine. She insists they help her get into character while also keeping her body limber. (Her character falls down the stairs in Act Two so flexibility is key.)

"How did your audition go?" I ask Jodie, eager to hear all about it. Everyone's always complaining about auditioning, but that's only because they get to audition all the time. I *wish*. Hearing about them after the fact is all I've got for now. But the moment mice are allowed to audition, you'd better bet I'll be ready.

"Well." Jodie completes her final lunge with a flourish and collapses onto the suede *chaise longue*. (That's French for a couch/chair combo.) "For starters, they were running behind."

"Of course," H.H. says, pinning down curl number nine. "He's *always* behind." She's referring to a director whose name I will not mention, because, well, I know better.

"Nancy Casey was sitting next to me and would not shut up about her one-day guest spot on that new CBS lawyer show."

"Typical." H.H. huffs. "Nancy Casey is a ridiculous human being." H.H. was married to a guy named Dave, and now Nancy Casey is married to a guy named Dave. (Same Dave, FYI.)

"Then, when I finally get into the room, do I get a 'Hello, Jodie, so lovely to see you. I just love the show. You were snubbed at the Tonys!' No, no. That Professor Snape wannabe stares blankly at me with his coal-colored eyes and says, 'What are you going to sing?' That's it, just, 'What are you going to sing?' like I'm not a two-time Tony nominee, three-time Drama Desk *winner*."

"Geez," I say. I mean, what else is there to say to an exquisite rant like that?

"Then—look at me when I say this, ladies," Jodie commands. H.H. and I do as we're told, obviously. When a sassy blonde tornado tells you to do something, you do it. "During my entire song, a song for which I received a standing ovation at Carnegie Hall, they did *not* look *up* from *the* TABLE!"

Then Heather Huffman says a word I would get soooooo punished for if I repeated, and Jodie goes, "I know!" followed by another only slightly less punishable word. Then, to further emphasize the sheer madness of it all, she puts both arms straight in front of her in a wide V, like she's going to hug a tree, fingers spread in a high five, à la Bob Fosse, and says, "And who goes into the room after me? That pinched gal from that BBC murder show. *Another Brit*. You heard it here first, ladies. The British aren't coming. They're already here."

"Fifteen Minutes. This is your Fifteen-Minute call. Fifteen Minutes, please," Pete's voice pipes over the intercom.

"Fifteen? How long have I been talking?!" Jodie flings off her clothes, and that's my cue to move on. Not like I'm embarrassed or anything. It's just polite.

"Have a good show!" I say, rolling H.H.'s Garnet Glory lipstick to her, my last task in our Tiny & H.H. preshow routine. We say, "Have a good show," or "Break a leg," but never "Good luck." That's bad luck. Weird, I know, but it's how it works in the theatre.

"Tiny, be a dear and tell Milly to tell that *adorable* Amanda that if she insists on stepping on my feet during bows I will be forced to *heavily* return the favor." Done with her pin curls, H.H. pulls her nude-colored wig cap over her head, secures it with a few bobby pins, and mutters, "Little brat." (P.S. A wig cap is basically a swim cap made out of pantyhose.)

"Will do!" I say, scampering down the arm of her dressing table and to the stairs, bound for the third floor. To Milly, who takes care of the kids and is, of course, awesome. To Maya, the understudy, who's sweeter than pie, and has the voice of an angel and the prettiest hair I've ever seen that isn't a wig. And Amanda. Ugh, Amanda. Okay, I'm going to be honest here. I do not like Amanda. I do not like her at all.

CHAPTER
THREE

O H MY *GEEZ*, LULU, YOU'RE *HERE*!" SHE MAY
sound sweet but don't be fooled. Amanda is
about as real as a gold-plated watch. (Quick
story: One of the male actors whom Heather Huffman
was "dating" gave her a gold-plated watch for her birthday. She called it a "cheap trinket of mediocrity" and
threw it down the stairs into the basement. It's now our
living room clock.)

"Ooooh what a pretty . . . *ribbon*, is it? It's so nice
that you make use of our scraps," Amanda says. See what
I mean? Sugarcoated meanness. "Isn't it pretty, Maya?"

"Really pretty, Lulu," Maya says.

Poor Maya. Long story short, Maya is Amanda's understudy, which means she plays the part Amanda plays when Amanda cannot. Maya has only performed the role twice in the ten months the show has been running, and that's only because Amanda was projectile vomiting into a bucket offstage right. And *people* think *mice* are gross. Honestly. Most of the time Maya just sits in the dressing room silently doing homework, fighting the urge—I can only assume—to poison Amanda with a bagel.

(Amanda has a "severe" gluten allergy. For all you celiac disease sufferers out there, please know I put "severe" in quotes for a reason. The reason being, I'm pretty sure she doesn't actually have a gluten allergy, but rather, a mother who doesn't want her daughter to eat "empty carbohydrates.")

"Thanks, guys. You're welcome to borrow it for your hair anytime," I say.

"Thanks, Lulu," Maya says, smiling sincerely.

"I'll pass," Amanda says. "It's not hygienic to share hair accessories."

Though she's probably right, why not just say, "Thanks, Lulu!" rather than, "I'll pass." I know what you're thinking, *Honesty is the best policy.* I see your "honesty is the best policy" and I raise you "if you don't have anything nice to say, don't say anything at all." Amanda isn't too familiar with that golden rule.

"Well, it's here if anyone wants it," I say. "Milly, may I speak with you privately for a moment?"

Milly—who's basically a real-life fairy, complete with sun-kissed hair, colorful clothing, and a cheery disposition—is sitting in the corner cross-legged, drinking a steaming chai tea out of her circa 1993 *Full House* thermos.

"Sure thing." Milly hops up.

The scoop on Milly? She's what we in the business call a "child wrangler" or "child guardian"—I've heard both terms used, so take your pick. Basically, Milly looks after the kids in the cast when they're at the theatre. (In this show, Amanda and Maya are the only kids.) Their parents drop them off at the stage door before Half Hour and pick them up when the show is over, with Milly taking care of them for the time in between. It's not like she's a babysitter or anything; Amanda and Maya are allowed to walk around the theatre without Milly following their every move. But it's Milly's job to make sure they make their entrances and exits, stay safe, and behave. Let's just say behavior isn't a problem for one out of the two of them.

"Not so fast. Whatever you can say in front of *Milly* you can say in front of me," Amanda declares.

Amanda is always saying things like this. Like she's some sort of queen or elected official. Luckily, Milly's a quick thinker. "Excuse me, but *someone* has a birthday coming up, so maybe *someone* should mind her own business and let us plan it, hmm?"

Upon hearing the magic word "birthday," Amanda grins like the Cheshire Cat from *Alice in Wonderland*

(Maybe that's why my stomach flips when I see her!) and goes back to applying her Strawberry Kiss blush. For the record, she wears way too much blush. She looks like a Cheshire Cat who rubbed its cheeks in a bucket of strawberry jam.

Milly carries me out to the hallway and places me on the windowsill. (If you're ever in Shubert Alley, look at the window three floors directly up from the stage door and that's where I am right now!)

I get carried and placed on high surfaces a lot around here; it's just easier that way. Less me looking up and them looking down. Everyone goes to enough physical therapy as it is, thanks to our never-ending stairwells and raked (read: slightly inclined) stage. The actors don't need neck problems because they've befriended a mouse.

"What's up?" Milly asks, twirling her dainty engagement ring. Sometimes she lets me try it on. I wear it as a crown. Her husband-to-be is in *The Phantom of the Opera* two theatres down at the Majestic. If you haven't seen it, go. A chandelier falls from the ceiling! I have cousins who live there. In the ceiling, not the chandelier. Obviously. A few months ago, after a family gathering, my mom and I watched the show from a crack in the wall of the mezzanine. Heaven.

"Heather Huffman asked me to ask you to ask Amanda to 'stop stepping on her feet or she'll be forced to heavily return the favor.' Direct quote."

"Goodness. I've told Amanda at least ten times," Milly says. "Maybe I should just let Heather step on her and see if that gets her to stop. Amanda has got to learn that the whole world doesn't revolve around her."

"Yeah," I say. What I want to say is, "She probably thinks it revolves around her because her face is plastered all over Shubert Alley and she was on all the morning shows plus *The Late Show with Stephen Colbert* before she turned twelve, and, man, I wish I were her." But instead I just say, "She won't always be the star." And I hope, hope, hope this is true. Because people like her don't deserve to be the star. Stars set the tone for the entire show, the mood for the entire building. They're someone youngsters like me look up to. Luckily, our grown-up star, Tony Award winner Stella James, is the nicest, most professional lady you'll ever meet, so she balances out Amanda's ickiness. More on Stella later . . .

"You certainly are wise for your age, Lulu," Milly says. Notice, she doesn't say, "for a mouse." She doesn't see me as a mouse, as something different and, therefore, scary or unequal. She sees me as a friend. A trusted friend.

I sure am lucky to have been born into a building of special, open-minded people. I could have ended up in an apartment building or (gulp) a restaurant and this would have been a shorter, scarier, and far less amusing story.

"Can you do something for me, if you don't mind?" Milly asks.

"Of course!" I say. I'd scurry all the way to Central Park if Milly asked. Not that I'm allowed to, but it's the thought that counts.

"Spend a little time with Maya during the show tonight?" she says. "I don't know how to tell you this, so I'll just pull off the metaphorical Band-Aid and say it. Maya is going to be leaving us in two weeks."

I'm pretty sure I audibly gasp. "What? Why? What happened?" I say. If this is Amanda's doing, so help me I will find an extra-gluten-full bagel (or something she's *actually* allergic to), convince the Hooligans to carry it up to the third floor, and force feed it to her myself.

"Her parents can't handle the drive from New Jersey anymore. They were okay with it at first because they thought she'd get to perform more often. But you know Amanda; she never misses a show." Milly's usual glow is fading. Like a firefly with its light out. I can tell she's genuinely upset for Maya. I am, too. This is super duper unfair. Amanda should be the one to go. If we put this to a vote, everyone in the theatre would vote for Maya to stay. Even you would vote for Maya at this point, right? Of course, right. (That's almost a direct quote from Yente in *Fiddler on the Roof*. She's highly quotable, FYI.)

"That's so sad. I feel so bad for her." I peer into the dressing room. Maya is gently caressing one of the costumes, the blue sparkly one. It's my favorite, and hers, too, I'm guessing, because she's touching it like she loves it more than anything in the world.

Then I hear Amanda say, "Maya. Stop. You *know* you're not supposed to touch the costumes unless you're in them. That's the *rule*." Ugh. Do be quiet, Amanda. That is not the rule and you know it.

I wish I would say that. I wish Maya would say that. She should stand up for herself. Heather Huffman is always saying, "It's necessary to teach others how you expect to be treated." I think she's mostly referring to boyfriends and talent agents, but I feel like it applies to mean girls as well.

But Maya says nothing. She just drops the dress. Like she's being forced to drop a barely licked ice-cream cone in the trash or something. Dropping her dream is more like it. It's heartbreaking to watch. And although *technically* I've never been in her shoes, I think I know how she feels. The only thing worse than losing a dream is not having a shot at it in the first place.

"What's going on, girls?" Milly asks, as if she doesn't already know. She's really good at treating them equally— even though she obviously *loves* Maya and only *likes* Amanda, because it's her job and she's a nice person.

She plops me down into Maya's sad lap. Yes, laps can be sad. Promise. Sad laps are the ones that are just begging you to sit in them.

"Nothing, Milly," Amanda says, batting her inexpertly applied eyelashes. She insists on wearing grown-up-sized lashes even though they're far too big for her kid-sized lash lines, so it looks like some sort of spider is crawling up her eyelid.

Amanda shoots a look to Maya as if to say, *Go ahead, say something, I dare you*, and it is moments like these that make me wish I could straighten out my tail and have it double as a magic wand. I'd turn Amanda into a pumpkin or a toad faster than you can say "bibbidi-bobbidi-boo."

"Five Minutes, this is your Five-Minute call. Five Minutes, please," Pete's voice booms from the monitor. Pete's voice is like what coffee would sound like if it could talk. Comforting, warm, yet still assertive and full of life.

Speaking of Pete, I guess this is as good of a time as any to meet a few of the people who work at my theatre-house. There are a lot of them. A lot. It's a safe bet to say that for each person onstage, there's someone offstage whose job is just as important. Remember that the next time you go see a Broadway show and wonder why your ticket is so expensive. I wouldn't know; I've never bought one because I get to watch for free, it being my own house and all. I just hear audience members complaining all the time, and it drives me kind of nuts.

So: there are the actors. Duh. You've met a few of them; you'll meet more. Then there's Pete. He's what's called the production stage manager. He basically runs things, now that the director has moved on to a different job. Pete's the one who makes sure everyone gets to the theatre on time and that the show starts when it's supposed to and ends when it's supposed to. He also gives acting notes to make sure the performances stay in tip-top shape. Then there are Ricardo and Susie. Ricardo is the assistant stage manager and Susie is the dance captain. Ricardo takes over for Pete when he's not around and Susie makes sure everyone continues to do the dance steps and blocking correctly. All three of them run understudy rehearsal every week. That's when, well . . . it's when the understudies rehearse. I guess that's pretty obvious.

I *always* attend understudy rehearsal. Sometimes I even help out, reading lines if an actor's missing. It's as close as I've ever gotten to actually being in a Broadway show.

Stop the train. Stop the music. Stop everything. (That's a quote from an incredible musical called *Gypsy*, which is loaded with kids but is also about a grown-up topic, so please check in with a legal guardian before you see it or watch one of the movie versions.) I can't believe I haven't gotten back to this since page 4! Thanks for continuing to read, by the way. I guess I'm an actress *and* a writer now. It seems wise to have multiple skills and interests. Show business is an uncertain path full of highs and lows, hills and valleys, sunshine and clouds . . . but still . . .

I want to be on Broadway. Onstage, up there, in front of the audience. I want to feel what it's like to be blinded by the lights; I want to make 'em laugh and make 'em cry. To sing. To dance. To bow. Oooooh do I wanna bow.

I used to say, "When I grow up, I want to be on Broadway." But then ten months ago, this show moved in, and Amanda and Maya are pretty young, and I realized that if they're old enough, I sure am. So, I cut out the "When I grow up" and started saying, "I want to be on Broadway."

Heather Huffman calls it a "positive affirmation."

Here's the thing, though. In case you'd forgotten. I know I'm eloquent and funny and it's easy to forget . . .

I'm a mouse. A darn cute and talented one but, well, mice can't be on Broadway. At least, none of us ever have been. I know it's not fair. It's just the way it is.

True, plenty of things never happened until they did. No one had ever walked on the moon until that Neil Armstrong guy did it. Apparently, telephones weren't a thing for a long time, which seems hard to believe. And my brother Benji couldn't say "Lucy Louise" until he was older than he'd care to admit. But things happened, and then they weren't so scary anymore. They weren't so . . . what's the word? Unattainable? Because they'd been attained. They'd happened. So what's to say I can't be the first mouse ever to perform on Broadway, right?

Wrong. According to my parents. My brothers. They're not mean about it; they just "don't want me to be heartbroken" when it doesn't happen.

"I wish I could fix it for you," my dad had said. "I wish I had the power to change it."

"No parent wants to tell her child something is impossible," my mother had said. "Anything is possible, I suppose. I just want to make sure you realize that a mouse performing on Broadway isn't probable, and I want you to be prepared for the disappointment."

"We'll start our own theatre!" Benji had said. "Who needs Broadway? We'll have Mouseway, Lulu; it'll be way better."

Though I knew he was just trying to make me feel better, I promptly told him that if I ever heard him say, "Who needs Broadway" ever again, I'd scream, "I NEED BROADWAY!" directly in his face.

Even Pete and I have talked about it. I asked him once, after understudy rehearsal, if maybe one day someone would give me a real shot, up there, in front of a real, live, paying audience. He was nice about it, of course. He picked me up, put me on his shoulder, and said, "Lulu, I'm going to be honest with you because you're my friend, and I'm always honest with my friends. The way the people in this theatre think? The way they think of you? They don't see you as a mouse. They see you as a little kid, and a talented one at that; you know this show just as well as they do, if not better. But most people? Regular people? They're just too closed-minded and ignorant to understand. They'd be scared. And we can't have audiences being scared because they might never come back."

Heavy, I know. But I get it. It's why my mom won't let me outside by myself. She's afraid of what would happen if a regular person saw me. I don't need to tell you what they might do; this isn't the eleven o'clock news.

All I'll say is: there's *never* any harm in dreaming that things and people and the world will change. And until they do, I'm darn grateful I'm surrounded by a bunch of humans who love me and treat me with respect. Well, maybe not Amanda. But she's not particularly nice to anyone, so I think the way she treats me is less about me being a different species and more about her and her own issues.

Anyway, "Enough of this boo-hooing!" as Jodie would say. Let's get back to the people who make this show possible. Long story short, we've got the actors, stage managers, backstage crew, carpenters, sound department, hair department, wardrobe department, Shubert employees—including our stage door people, box office workers, cleaning staff, concessions and merchandise staff, security guards. . . . What's important is to remember that it takes a team, a village, a *family* to put on a Broadway show and take care of the theatre. One person is removed and the whole thing collapses like a Jenga tower.

If this were my Tony Award acceptance speech, I'd probably say something like, "A big shout-out and endless thanks to my Shubert Theatre family. This show couldn't happen without you. But more than that, I wouldn't be who I am without you."

I may or may not practice that speech every night before I go to bed.

Okay, let's get back to what's actually happening right now, only a few short minutes before our Tuesday performance begins.

"Jeremiah! Owwwwwwww, that *hurts*," Amanda screams. Before you call the cops, let me explain. Jeremiah is pinning on Amanda's wig. Because, as head of the hair department, it's his job to style, maintain, and handle the wigs. He also pins on Heather Huffman's and Jodie's wigs and they never even flinch. That's because he uses rubber-coated metal hairpins and not flaming fireplace pokers like Amanda's making it seem. It's painless. She's a big fat phony. Let's continue.

"Sorry, Amanda," Jeremiah says. He adjusts a pin. "Better?"

"A little. You need to be more careful. The brain is very important." She's not joking. She's not anywhere near joking. Wait until I tell Heather Huffman and Jodie

Howard that Amanda said something ridiculous like, "The brain is very important." I can already hear Jodie's response. "No shoot, Sherlock," she'll say. Followed by a harmonious, "Good lord," from both of them.

Also, can we all acknowledge that Jeremiah hitting Amanda's brain with a two-inch bobby pin is physically impossible? I'm a mouse-kid and even I know there's a skull and a bunch of layers of goop to get through before you get to the actual brain.

"Yep. Sorry. Won't happen again," Jeremiah says as Amanda slithers out of the room. "Until tomorrow," he says. "Because no matter how careful I am, she complains."

"I know," Milly says. "I'll have another chat with her."

"Don't bother," Jeremiah says. "I've been to enough therapy to know that you can't change another person. You can only change your reaction to that person." Then he turns to Maya, his face shifting from frustration to disappointment. "Well, Miss Maya. I hear you're leaving us soon. Worst news I've heard all week."

"Yeah," she says. "The drive is just too much for my parents. Plus, balancing it with school has been really tough." If you need help envisioning the painfully upsetting look on her face, just picture your face that Christmas morning when you asked for a puppy and got socks.

"Maybe you'll get to go on one more time," I say.

Jeremiah shoots me this look that basically says, *Youthful hope is so adorable.*

"Maybe," Maya says. "I doubt it. You know Amanda."

"Unfortunately," I blurt. You know the saying, "Think before you speak"? Sometimes that's just not possible.

"Whoa, Lulu!" Jeremiah says. "Tell us how you really feel."

"Sars I'm not sars," I say. I learned this from Chris in wardrobe. Eighty percent of what Chris says is cute little catchphrases. "Sars I'm not sars" is Chris-speak for, "Sorry I'm not sorry." Cute, right? (A bit of advice? Don't say it to your parents or teachers or any other authority figure. I speak from personal experience: it won't go well.

Stick to your pals. They'll think it's cool.)

Maya giggles. It feels good to make her laugh. "You're the best, Lulu. I'm really going to miss you," she says.

Now I'm the one who needs a laugh. We're one good cry away from Dorothy saying her goodbyes at the end of *The Wizard of Oz*.

"Places, please, for the top of Act One. This is your Places call. Places, please," Pete's voice booms over the monitor.

It's not a laugh; it's better. It's Places. When everyone takes their, well . . . places, for the top of the show. The beginning. I just love it.

Technically, our show starts as most musicals do: with an overture—bits of each song from the show's score, played only by the orchestra—but the majority of the company is in the show's opening scene, which immediately follows the overture. So Places means "get to the stage as the overture is beginning so Pete can make sure you're ready for your first entrance." There are a few characters who don't appear in the show until Act Two, and those actors usually use the Places call as their cue to begin getting ready for the show—prepping their hair, doing their makeup, that sort of thing.

Milly pops her head into the dressing room. "It's Places, ladies. Let's get this show on the road."

Here's one of the best things about the theatre versus television or film: the same thing happens every night, with teeny tiny differences scattered all over the place. Everything is set in stone, but we prepare for slight alterations because that's just the nature of live theatre.

The audience makes a difference: if they're particularly vocal or eager to applaud, if they're super quiet, if a cell phone goes off (*turn your cell phones off, people!*) all these things can affect a performance.

Then there's the stuff onstage and backstage. If an understudy is on, things are inevitably a little different. Every now and then, whether or not there are understudies involved, someone will make a mistake like flubbing a line or forgetting a prop. Once, one of the actors accidentally missed an entrance because he was watching the World Series, and needless to say we no longer have a television in the basement. But overall, it's one big routine. And one of our routines is our overture dance.

While the musicians play, the curtain is down so the audience can't see us, and we just go to town, our dancing fueled by the mischievous joy of knowing there's an audience on the other side of the curtain who has no idea we're doing what we're doing. We can be as loud as we want because there's no way we'll ever be louder than our twenty-four-piece orchestra, especially since the cast's microphones haven't been turned on yet.

The chorus members do splits and kicks; one of them does this really funny dance called the "hottie dottie" that involves a second position plié and swinging arms. (It's a hoot, promise.) At the end, we all do the bunny hop, which everyone has renamed "the mouse hop." Even though mice don't hop, I love them for the thought. Maya and I have our own little routine that involves me sitting on her shoulder and . . . oh.

She's leaving. Who am I going to dance with? We've done three hundred and twenty-two overture dances. And after this performance, we'll only do fifteen more.

Oh my goodness, oh my goodness! (Direct quote: *Annie.* Specifically, one of the orphans named Tessie. Please tell me you've seen the movie. Carol Burnett as Miss Hannigan? I can't even.) It just hit me. Not only is Maya going to leave, but someone new is going to take her place.

Who will she be, I wonder? Will she be kind, polite, and super talented like Maya? Will she be younger? Will she be older? Will she be my friend, or Amanda's? She won't fall for Amanda's sugarcoated cruelty, will she? What if she's just like Amanda? What if she's worse? Whoever she is, like it or not, two weeks from today, she'll be here, and Maya will not.

One of the things about theatre folk that's both frustrating and wonderful at the same time is we bond super quickly; we become more than friends—we become family. We get used to one another, fall into a routine. We can't imagine not being around one another six days a week. And then one day, something changes. Someone leaves, or even worse, the show closes. This is the fifth show to inhabit this theatre during my lifetime, the seventh since my parents have lived here. A show closes, a new cast and a mostly new crew moves in; the new show takes the old one's place. We're left with memories and stories and, hopefully, friendships.

But tell me, what kind of career requires falling in love with a group of people, bonding, working together six days a week, and then abruptly abandoning all of it for another job? Or worse . . . unemployment. I know I'm just a mouse, but I think about all of these things. It breaks my heart when cast members of the show that closed last year come back to visit and say they haven't worked since. And as a fellow performer, it scares me. Being an artist means years of inconsistency, change, and unabashed commitment to one's art!

Whoa, now. This is all getting wayyyyy too serious. We're too young for this level of anxiety. It's hottie dottie time, fo' sho'. (That's Chris talk for "for sure.")

I'm in Maya's palms as we make our way downstairs for Places and the overture dance, following Jeremiah and Milly. Heather Huffman and Jodie join our parade; they're still talking about Jodie's audition. Jodie flails her arms around for emphasis. "It's a gee-dee miracle they didn't ask me to dance. Can you imagine?"

"I can. It wouldn't be pretty," H.H. replies.

"Heather, did I ever mention that I saw you play Miss Adelaide in *Guys and Dolls*?" Jeremiah asks. He has mentioned it before. I was there when he mentioned it. I think he just likes reliving the experience. *Guys and Dolls* is a fabulous show.

"No!" H.H. exclaims. I guess she likes reliving it, too.

"Oh my goodness, you must have been a baby."

"I was fourteen. But I still knew a star when I saw one," Jeremiah says with a smile that makes the dimple in his left cheek . . . dimple. "Your dancing in 'A Bushel and a Peck' was something to see." Jeremiah dates men but is "such a flirt," according to *everyone*.

"That show was a dream. Oh, Tiny, I wish you could have seen it," H.H. says.

"I do, too!" I say. Pretty sure I said that last time this scene played out.

"I was—"

"Fabulous, but far too young for the role," Jodie finishes.

"When you're right, you're right," H.H. says, linking arms with Jodie, the two ladies cackling like non-scary witches.

We land by the stage door, right in front of the sign-in sheet and Rosa, our night doorwoman. She's been working at the Shubert since the eighties. My parents say she has looked exactly the same since they met her many, many years ago, and because of this, Walt and Matty did their best to convince me that she's a ghost. Nice try, big brothers, but I'm certain she's not a ghost. Not because I don't believe in ghosts, but because I'm pretty sure ghosts can't leave the theatre and go across the street to get iced coffee and bagels with lox and a schmear.

"What's all this noise? Don't you people know there's a Broadway show about to begin?" Rosa snaps.

She's kidding, obviously. She's always pretend-scolding people, and sometimes real-scolding. When she's real-scolding, you'd better watch out. She doesn't take any shenanigans from anyone. Not even our—

Star. There she is. Stella James, in the flesh, heading out of her private dressing room, a room that smells like lilacs and fresh laundry. I swear, every time I see her I get a little dizzy. I never know what to say. I get completely tongue-tied, and you know me by now: finding my words is not usually a problem. She has two Tony Awards, she's been in movies and on television, and she performs concerts all over the world. She's my idol. And she's small, for a human. Five feet, two inches on the dot. Does that stop her? No, it does not.

"Hello, everyone," she says, followed by her dresser, Chris.

"Hey, y'all," Chris says. He's not even from the South but he still says "y'all." How cool is that?

"Why, Lulu," Stella says. "Isn't that a becoming accessory."

I gulp. She's talking about my chartreuse ribbon-scarf. She likes my chartreuse ribbon-scarf. Sits-front-row-at-Fashion-Week Stella James likes *my* chartreuse ribbon-scarf. Don't faint, Lulu. Don't get tongue-tied. Just say thank you. Say thank you.

"Thanks, Stella." (FYI, I called her Ms. James until she repeatedly told me it wasn't necessary.) "It's chartreuse," I say. Like she didn't know that already. Uggghhhhh.

"It certainly is," she says. "Very becoming." And she *pats me on the head*. "Have a good show, everyone."

Everyone says their good shows back, and she's off, with Chris trailing behind her. He turns around, points to my scarf, and whispers, *"Fierce."* He usually saves his "fierces" for a particularly expensive purse or someone's brand-new, "bank-breakingly natural" highlights. I got a pat on the head from Stella and a "fierce" from Chris. What is this, my birthday?!

My spell of happiness is instantly broken by the fact that Maya has started to cry. Nothing too loud or dramatic, just real and heartbreaking. She wipes away a single tear, the kind of tear television actors dream of.

"What's wrong?" I ask. Even though I'm pretty sure I know.

"I can't believe I only have two weeks left," Maya says, leaning into Milly, who's doing her best not to cry, too.

"I know, honey," Milly says, hugging her close.

"This is just the beginning for you, Maya," Jeremiah says.

"And this stage door is always open to you," Rosa chimes in. "Anytime you're walking by, I expect you to say hello." All of this is making Maya cry even more, so Jodie does what she does best. She dumps a big bucket of sass on the flames of sadness.

"Look on the bright side, honey," Jodie says. "At least you won't have to put up with Little Miss All-About-Me anymore. I swear, the next contract I sign, I'm having them put a no-Amanda clause in it." For the record, Jodie and the rest of the cast tried very hard to be nice to Amanda for the first five or six months of the run, but even grown-ups can only put up with so much.

Maya smiles and, like the classy young lady she is, says, "Amanda's not that bad."

Jodie looks at Maya with a serious stare and says, "I'd rather pluck my eyelashes out one by one than share a dressing room with her. You're a saint."

On cue, Amanda appears. "Did someone say my name?"

"Yep," Heather Huffman says, shooting Amanda her best *don't mess with me, kid* glare.

"Why?" Amanda asks, with the bite of an extra-sharp block of cheddar. "Who said it and what was said?" She's so paranoid. For good reason, I suppose, but still.

"I was just saying how much I'm going to miss everyone," Maya says. "Including you." And although I'm sure she's saying it mostly to appease Amanda, I think a little part of Maya means it. Like it or not, Amanda was a part of Maya's Broadway debut. Their histories are forever linked. Amanda may have tortured her, but she did it in a Broadway theatre. Things could be worse. All of this animosity could have happened somewhere regular, like sixth grade or karate class.

"Oh my *geez*, look at you, you're *crying*." Amanda puts her arms around Maya, enveloping her in an elaborate hug. "You poor thing."

I swear to you, Amanda's looking around waiting for someone to congratulate her on being such a good pal. Obviously, no one takes the bait. Instead, Heather Huffman throws out a "I'll never forget the times you went on, Maya. You're a real talent. Know that and own it."

If there's one thing Amanda hates, it's being reminded that she puked in a bucket and then missed two shows. If there's another thing Amanda hates, it's hearing that Maya is super talented. She instantly breaks the hug, turns on a dime, and barks, "The overture's starting soon. You know I can't miss my preshow," then stomps onto the stage.

"What's amusing is she thinks we can't see through her nonsense," H.H. says. "But karma is real. I've been in this business longer than I care to admit, and I promise you, people like Amanda always get back what they've given out, tenfold."

And with those words of wisdom, the orchestra starts to play, and we all find our way to the stage and our overture dance.

CHAPTER
FOUR

THIRTY-FIVE MINUTES INTO THE SHOW, I CREEP
downstairs, hoping to sneak into my nest without
anyone noticing. My "quiet as a mouse" routine
doesn't come close to working, because my mother, like all
mothers, hears everything.

"Do my ears deceive me, Lucy Louise, or is it well
past the first number?" My mother is standing with her
hip popped and her whiskers straight out, which means
she means business.

"I had to stay a little while longer, Mom. Maya was
really upset." A word to the wise: if you ever disobey your
parents, you'd better make sure it's for a good, moral reason.

"What did Amanda do this time?" my mother asks, her whiskers relaxing a bit, genuinely concerned. She does *not* like the fact that Amanda gets away with such bad behavior. She blames Amanda's mother, who, she says, "acts more like a friend than a parent." My mother takes parenting *very* seriously.

"Amanda didn't do anything out of the ordinary," I say.

"So is this about Maya leaving the show?" my mom asks, folding the freshly washed fabric scraps we use as our bedding.

"You knew?" I ask. "Why didn't you tell me?"

"I overheard Bet and Pete talking about it," she says. "I didn't think it was my place to say."

"Well," I say, "Maya is really upset."

"And so are you," Mom says.

"And so am I. I'm going to miss her. And . . . ," I start.

"And what?" Mom asks.

"And what if the new girl and Amanda get along and

I get left out? It's already so ridiculous that Amanda gets the lead role, even though Maya is just as talented and much nicer. Maya should be the one to stay and Amanda should go," I rant. "It's just not fair."

"Life's not always fair, my love," Mom says, bringing me a bottle cap full of hot chocolate—my fave. "And worrying about the new girl won't do you any good. Worrying doesn't help anything. All you can do is be the Lucy Louise I raised you to be. Treat the new girl the way you'd want to be treated. And even though it's difficult, try to go easy on Amanda."

"Ick. Why?" I ask. This hot chocolate is to die for, by the way. My mom makes it out of the concession stand M&M's that audience members drop on the floor.

"People like Amanda, their outward meanness is usually masking a much deeper insecurity. Truly confident people don't need to put others down to lift themselves up." I think of our show's star, Stella James, and realize this is true. I've never heard her say a bad word about anyone, and she's the most confident person I know. Even if she thinks bad thoughts, she certainly never says them out loud. "I'm sure the new girl will be lovely, and if she happens not to be, well then, you'll be lovely enough for the both of you."

"I guess," I say. My mom is *so* right, but there's no reason to make a big deal about it.

"And in the meantime? Sewing, bath, bed," she instructs.

Ugh, when she's right, she's right. I nod, and meander toward my nest, wishing I could skip sewing practice and go straight to bath and bed. Or better yet: bow, bath, bed. Something to dream about, I suppose.

CHAPTER
FIVE

WEDNESDAY WAS AS WEDNESDAYS USUALLY are: busy. We have a matinee at 2:00 and an evening show at 7:30, recently changed from 8:00, much to the chagrin of mostly everyone.

"Seven thirty?!" Jodie had exclaimed. "What is this, *Wheel of Fortune?*"

"This is ridiculous," H.H. had said when the shift happened. "Make it seven or eight o'clock, but seven thirty will just cause confusion."

And sure enough, theatregoers often show up early, assuming the show is at 7:00, which makes for a box office full of angry audience members who "rushed through dinner at Becco!"—and a super full Starbucks around the corner. Or they'll arrive late, thinking the show begins at 8:00, and according to those up on the stage, watching and listening to people shuffle to their seats in the dark while you're trying to sing and stay in character is *très* distracting.

Amanda had a little bit of a cough by the end of Tuesday's show but promptly told Maya "not to get her hopes up." Amanda's mother had her doctor on speed dial (the poor guy), and by noon on Wednesday, Amanda had already seen him and been prescribed a throat-numbing spray, which required a signed waiver since it's pending approval by the FDA.

Anyway, Amanda had added, she was pretty sure she'd gotten the cough from Maya's little brother who had the sniffles the week before and *technically* he isn't allowed backstage and Milly should *really* enforce the rules and STOP MAKING THINGS UP, AMANDA.

By Wednesday night, I was even more exhausted

than I usually am on two-show days because my mom had let me spend all of both shows with Maya, knowing how upset she was, and that we only had two weeks left together. Less than two weeks: thirteen shows by the end of Wednesday. Ugh.

Even the Hooligans made an appearance up in the dressing room, which is a rare occurrence seeing as Walt and Matty spend most of their free time scurrying around in the alley between our theatre and the Broadhurst, Timmy found a pile of old copies of *Variety* into which he has permanently buried his nose, and Benji has started to help Pete and Ricardo with the "show reports" because he can type one hundred words per minute—using his feet. Yes, while I'm the only one in the family who prefers hanging out with the cast to just about anything else, my brothers made it a point to visit Maya because she's just that great.

"I'll sneeze on Amanda! Right on her. Get her sick in no time," Walt had offered.

"Yeah," Matty joined in, "he'll sneeze on her and I'll cough. And Benji'll mess with her dressing room humidifier, won't you, Benj?"

"Consider it done," Benji had said, in a dead-serious tone.

"You guys are too sweet," Maya had said, tears welling up in her throat. She was even going to miss my hooligan brothers, the dear girl. And whether they admit it or not, they're going to miss her, too. Especially Benji. Judging by how often he talks about her hair, I'm pretty sure he's in love.

This is an actual conversation I overheard last week between Benji and Maya. I suppose I'll take this opportunity to exercise my playwriting skills.

THE SETTING: *The third-floor hallway, right outside of the bathroom*

THE DAY: *Friday*

THE TIME: *Ten minutes to Half Hour*

A toilet flushes. Exiting the bathroom, MAYA *enters the hallway. She's just had a haircut, so her curls are particularly bouncy. She spots* BENJI, *who pretends to inspect a speck of dirt on the wall, to make it seem like he wasn't waiting for her.*

MAYA   Hey, Benji. What's up?

BENJI   You look beautiful.

MAYA   Oh. You're so sweet. Thank you.

BENJI   Your hair is like golden silk.

MAYA   Oh. Um. Thanks.

BENJI   You smell like almonds.

MAYA   Ummmm . . . Thank you?

Benji nervously farts and scurries off.

End scene

I wake up early Thursday afternoon—I'm in show business and I'm a mouse, so I usually sleep late—in anxious anticipation of the afternoon's understudy rehearsal. It will be the first time we'll all meet Maya's replacement.

Pete assured us she was "the best of the best." As production stage manager, he'd been at her audition and was "really impressed by her." He says she's "the real deal."

Of course, I'd expect nothing less than the best of the best or the real deal—this is *Broadway*, after all. What I'm concerned about is her personality. Will she be Maya-like or Amanda-like?

"Perhaps she'll just be *herself*," my mother says. She's sitting on a spool of fuchsia thread with a needle across her lap. She unravels a bit of the thread and bites it (because who needs scissors when you've got mouse teeth!), then sticks the thread through the needle's eye, knotting the loose ends with efficient ease.

"Here you are, Bet," Mom says. In case you couldn't guess, we're in the wardrobe room, helping Bet with "day work"—laundry, repairs, and inventory. Being Bet's assistant is my mom's actual job. She doesn't get paid in money, because we mice don't have any need for human money (though I once used an old dollar bill as a summer blanket and I've gotta say, it was the perfect combination of soft and breathable). Instead, Bet pays my mother in food and supplies for our home. I'm in training to join the wardrobe staff someday—hence the sewing homework— but I think it's pretty clear it's not my dream job. Nothing to do with Bet, of course. She's absolutely wonderful. It's just that, well . . . sewing doesn't hold a candle to performing. (Duh.)

"Bless you and your tiny feet," Bet says to my mom, then turns to me. "Without your mother, I'd spend most of my day attempting to thread needles. My eyes aren't what they used to be."

Bet, by the way, is literally the oldest person in the theatre. "I'm older than the ghosts," she always says. (Side note: Aside from my brothers attempting to trick me into thinking Rosa is a ghost, I've never actually encountered one, but apparently there are ghosts in Broadway theatres. Ghosts of actors and writers and such, though, so nothing scary.)

Bet is a first-generation Italian American. (Yes, she fulfills the stereotype and is an excellent cook. Just the thought of her eggplant parmesan makes my mouth water. The crunchy, almost burnt bits around the edge of the pan? Yes, please, and thank you.) Her parents came over on a boat from Italy around the turn of the twentieth century and had ten kids once they got here—eight girls and two boys. Bet is the youngest and the only one still living. She's *ninety*. I'm not kidding. *Ninety*. As in, ten less than one hundred. But you'd never know it. She's as sharp as a sewing needle, and speaking of sewing needles, you should see her with one. She's an artist. "She epitomizes work ethic," my mother always says. Bet is my mother's Heather Huffman.

Bet was also—so the legend says—the first person in the theatre to befriend a mouse. Let's take a moment away from the present to "journey to the past," as they say in *Anastasia*, so you can learn Bet's incredible story.

AFTER HER TWO BROTHERS DIED IN WORLD WAR II, TEEN-age Bet took it upon herself to get a job since her brothers were no longer there to help out. She'd always been a skilled seamstress, so she figured she might as well make money at it, to help her family put food on the table. That's how things worked in those days: the men went off to work and the women stayed home. But not Bet. She was a pioneer. (Like I'd like to be, you know?)

Carolina, one of Bet's sisters, was a fantastic dancer, and a producer had approached her at a local dance hall with an offer for a job in the chorus of a Broadway musical called Bloomer Girl that was opening at the Shubert. Bet's parents—very traditional and wary of America, which was still a scary, new world to them—said, "Assolutamente no!" to Carolina's dancing on Broadway. But Carolina defied her parents and did it anyway. And her parents swore never to speak to her again.

In an effort to bring her family back together, Bet applied for a job as a seamstress at the Shubert so she could keep an eye on her sister and report back to her parents. She promised them that theatre people were wonderful and good; told them that Carolina was a beautiful dancer who worked very hard at her craft, and that if they just came to a performance, they could see for themselves and they could all be a family again. And they did. And they were.

During Bet's first week at the theatre, another seamstress spotted a mouse on a water pipe in the wardrobe room. The seamstress screamed and swatted at the mouse with a broom, promising to return the next day with mouse traps.

But Bet was different. When she turned on the light the next morning to find a mouse sitting on her Singer sewing machine, she didn't scream. Instead, she said, "Hello, there, little one. I'm Bet."

And the mouse replied, "I'm Poppy. A pleasure to meet you."

"May I assume, by the fact that you're sitting on my sewing machine, that you have an interest in sewing?" Bet had asked Poppy.

"It's my favorite thing," Poppy had said. "It's my dream to sew costumes for a Broadway show. But . . ."

"But?" Bet had asked, sitting down so she was face-to-face with Poppy.

"But it's just not done," Poppy had said.

"Well," Bet had replied, "there's a first time for everything."

And from that day forward, if any human swatted at a mouse or went to set a trap, Bet reminded them, "These mice are here to help us. They're our coworkers, not our enemies. Learn their names and be kind to them, and you'll quickly see your workload cut in half and your spirits lifted."

THAT CONCLUDES THE TALE OF HOW BET BECAME THE first human to befriend a Broadway mouse. I now return you to your regularly scheduled program: "Lulu Freaks Out about the New Girl."

"What if the new girl's 'being herself' is being mean to mice?" I ask.

"I suppose anything's possible," my mother says. "But why go into something assuming it won't work out?"

"Faith is greater than fear," Bet says. "Assume she'll be wonderful and deal with it later if she isn't. Her name is Jayne. With a *Y*. How could a Jayne with a *Y* be anything but a delight?"

"Pretty name," my mother says.

"I guess," I reply, pacing across the washing machine. I don't understand why having a (sometimes) vowel in your name automatically means you'll be delightful, but Bet is usually right about things, so I see no point in quibbling.

Bet shows me a mesh laundry bag with Jayne's name on it. In the theatre, we call this a "ditty bag." At the beginning of the show, it's full of clean "personal" laundry—socks, underwear, bras, and such—and at the end of the show, the actors fill it with their newly worn, dirty laundry. I'd let the Hooligans step on my tail twenty times over in exchange for my own ditty bag complete with my own show undergarments, thank you. I'm not asking for much; the bag would be smaller than a Post-it.

"And did I mention," Bet says, "she's getting her own costumes because she's quite a bit smaller than Amanda and Maya."

"Really?" I high-kick with glee. Amanda will not be happy about that. Height is a sensitive subject for her. It is a known fact that the moment Amanda gets anywhere near Stella's height, she'll be replaced. It's in her contract and everything. She's taken to slouching during the one scene where Stella wears flat shoes. As I said earlier, Stella's on the small side for a grown-up.

"Really," Bet says. "She's a peanut, like you."

"Company to the stage for understudy rehearsal, please. Company to the stage for understudy rehearsal." Pete's voice sounds like an extra frothy cappuccino today. Scratch that: a seasonal latte with an extra pump of pumpkin.

"Looks like your wait is over, Lucy Louise," my mom says as I scurry across a ceiling water pipe—my most direct route upstairs.

"Be sure to report back," Bet requests, pressing START on the washing machine whose lid I recently vacated. (I learned at a young age not to walk on a running washing machine. It's the mouse version of an amusement park ride gone wrong.)

"Oh, I will," I say. And I make my way upstairs.

Between you and me, my stomach is in knots. What I haven't been able to admit to anyone is that I'm not just worried about the energy shift the new girl will cause. What I'm feeling is different and possibly worse than worry. To quote Shakespeare's Iago, I'm dealing with "the green-eyed monster": envy.

I know Amanda's role like the back of my hand. To be honest, I know everyone's role like the back of my hand, but Amanda's is especially ingrained in me, because her character is the same age as I am, and, despite the fact that the character is played by Amanda, I love the part. *Love.* Her character is sassy, she's smart, she speaks French! It's perfect for me. I spend so many days alone in my nest practicing her songs and dance steps, and so many nights dreaming of a scenario that would lead to me performing her role. . . .

Maya could get stuck in New Jersey because of snow and Amanda could slip on the ice on her way into the theatre, her ankle too swollen to perform. Or they could both catch the same cold, which happens a lot in the theatre, forcing them both to stay home and recuperate in front of the TV, which is the only fun thing about having a cold. . . . Stella could see me at understudy rehearsal and insist that I go on, that my talent is too great not to share with the world. . . .

These are all just fantasies, I know. They're never going to happen. But that doesn't stop me from feeling deeply envious of the new girl. *Jayne.* The girl who will—hopefully, for her sake—get to make her Broadway debut at the most beautiful theatre on Broadway in one of the most beautiful shows of all time opposite one of the world's most beautiful and talented stars. I'm envious. It's not something I'm proud of, but it's the truth.

I arrive upstairs just as the understudies begin to assemble onstage. As I said, Wednesdays are long days, so it usually takes everyone a few minutes to pep up on understudy Thursdays.

I take my usual front row seat in the house—the house is what we call where the audience sits, by the way. I know it's confusing because the whole theatre is actually *my* house, but the house is what we call the audience seating area, so . . . that's what it's called, so . . . "Sorry 'bout it," as Chris would say.

I see Maya and Milly huddled onstage left. Then Pete walks out, followed by Susie and Ricardo, and they stand center stage. This is it. This must be the moment. The moment they introduce the new girl. *Jayne.* The girl I will do my best to be kind to, to be open-minded about, the girl I will try my hardest not to be envious of.

Where the heck is she, though? Being late on the first day isn't exactly a smart move.

"Let's settle, people, settle." Pete says this all the time. In case you couldn't tell, theatre people tend to be a chatty bunch. "As you all know, our dear Maya is leaving us in less than two weeks."

A few of the cast members look to one another and make frowny faces. I'm telling you: everyone loves Maya.

"We will, of course, miss her terribly. But the show must go on, and her replacement must be trained and ready."

"Like Amanda will ever take a show off," I hear Chris say as he saunters across the stage carrying freshly laundered costumes. "She's like an extra-strength energizer bunny." A few people laugh, and Pete shoots them a reprimanding look.

"I'm happy to introduce Miss Jayne Griffin. Let's everyone give her a round of applause." We all applaud,

and out from behind Milly and Maya steps a tiny girl. *Tiny.*
Teeny tiny. Think of the smallest girl you know and make
her smaller. She's the human version of a mouse. She's the
human version of me.

"Come on over, Jayne. Meet your fellow understudies,"
Pete says. He looks to Susie, who goes over and takes Jayne
by the hand, walking her to center stage (aka the best place
in the whole world).

The group applauds and cheers, and Jayne is smiling
but also looks like she's going to burst into tears/puke.

"Anything you'd like to say, Jayne?" Pete asks.

"I . . ." She's shaking. "I . . ."

Oh no. I've seen this look before. Five times, exactly,
during my life in the theatre. It's a look you can't forget
because it's impossible not to feel for the person wearing it.

Stage fright. I can see it's not our castmates who are the
cause. She's nervous to meet them, I'm sure, but it's standing
center stage that's getting to her. I don't get nervous—
it being my house and all—but I can imagine that looking

out into the house, with all its lights on, seeing all the empty seats, imagining all the audience members, all eyes on you. . . .

Okay, to be *honest*, thinking about all that makes me feel the opposite of nervous. The idea of it is super exciting for me, but Jayne's entitled to her own feelings, so back to her.

She's still solid as a statue.

"I . . . ," she manages.

This gal needs my help. If she doesn't snap out of it soon, I can imagine Pete reporting back to the director that she wound up "not cutting it," and then they'd replace her, and the only thing worse than never getting the opportunity to audition for a Broadway show has got to be getting the job and having it taken away on your first day.

I start to tap dance in an effort to get her attention. *Shuffle, ball change. Flap, flap.* It's part of the finale dance combo.

She spots me. Our eyes meet. *Shuffle, ball change, stomp, stomp.*

And she doesn't even flinch. Doesn't jump. Doesn't yell, "Help! A tap-dancing mouse!" She's one of us.

I smile, and she smiles. And her shaking stops. I take a deep breath, and she follows with a deep breath. (Sometimes, in between shows on Wednesdays, I do yoga with the dancers up in the balcony, so I know how helpful a simple, deep breath can be.)

I give her my best *you've got this, girl* nod and wink. She stands tall, turns to the group, and says, "I'm just so grateful to be here."

With this simple display of sincerity, everyone applauds some more.

"Sweet little thing," Chris says.

Milly and Maya smile with relief.

Pete and Susie laugh in a kind, parental way.

And I know. I know in that moment: Jayne and I are going to be great friends. The kind of friends who can tell each other anything. The kind of friends who can be themselves when they're together—cry, laugh, say it all without saying a word. The kind of friends who can help each other get through anything, even stage fright.

Then Pete hollers to get everyone's attention. (He never whistles. You *never* whistle in the theatre. It's a leftover superstition from back in the day when crew members used to whistle at one another as a cue to lower curtains and such. Now things are run by computers and cues over the sound system, but to honor tradition and be extra careful that no one gets hit on the head with an accidental curtain or flying set piece, we *never* whistle.)

The company settles into place to go over the opening number, and Jayne's first understudy rehearsal begins.

CHAPTER
SIX

JAYNE AND I ARE IN THE HOUSE, SITTING FRONT
row center, during our first ten-minute break of
understudy rehearsal. Maya and Milly have run off
to the bathroom, so it's just me and Jayne. Me and my
new friend, Jayne. Me and the gal I was afraid would be
awful but is actually a delight; so, yes, my mother and
Bet were right, per usual.

"So," Jayne says, "you can talk."

"You can talk, too, but you don't see me making a big
deal about it," I say with a smile.

Somewhere in the basement my mother is saying,
"Take the sass down a few notches, Lucy Louise."

"It's just . . . I didn't know that mice talking was a thing," Jayne says, almost apologetically.

"Most people don't know," I say.

"Is it some sort of theatre magic?" Jayne asks.

"No, we can talk everywhere," I say. "But so far, only theatre people listen."

"That's because they're the best people," Jayne says, staring up at the stage where a few cast members are lounging around in various dance stretches, laughing and smiling and being generally fantastic.

"I can't argue with you there," I say.

Then Jayne looks at the ceiling, her little body twisting so she can glance up and around toward the mezzanine and balcony, the awe and wonderment of it all making her face glisten like it's been sprinkled with fairy dust. When this show moved into the theatre, there were fourteen Broadway debuts in the cast. Watching them wander around, jaws practically on the ground, H.H. had said to me, "No matter how many dance lessons or drama classes a person takes, no matter how many auditions they go on or how many nights they lie awake thinking about it—nothing prepares them for the splendor that is their first day in a Broadway theatre, knowing it's no longer their dream, it's their reality." The quotable quotes that come out of that woman. I mean, really. She should write a book.

"I've dreamed of this, you know?" Jayne says, her big eyes tracing an arc around our gold-trimmed proscenium.

"Yeah, I know," I say. Little does she know how much I know. I briefly consider telling her that I, too, dream of the theatre, but this isn't about me; this is Jayne's moment. So, I don't say anything about how hard it is to live here and not be able to perform up on that stage. But it just felt darn good saying it to you! Anyway, back to Jayne.

"I've been going to dance class in the city for the last year or so. We live in the suburbs. Westchester County? Have you heard of it?" Apparently meeting a talking, tap-dancing mouse can make a gal particularly chatty. "Anyway, after tap class my dad takes me to the burger place by Saks for a tuna sandwich, onion rings, and a black-and-white shake, and then we walk the streets of the theatre district. It's my favorite day of the week."

"That sounds incredible," I say. I've heard of that burger place by Saks. Believe you me, we mice know where the good food is. And walking the streets of the theatre district with your dad? Um, sign me up. The farthest my dad and I have gotten is the corner of Forty-Fourth and Ninth and even that was thrilling. (By the way, great pizza on Forty-Fourth and Ninth. I bet it's even better pre–garbage can.)

"And now," Jayne says, "I'm here. I'm on Broadway *and* in my favorite theatre."

"Your favorite, huh?" I say with a smile. I knew I liked this girl.

"How could it not be? It's on its own corner, it has its own alley. *A Chorus Line* opened here! And those little windows up on the top floor? Are those apartments up there? I'd love to live there. Do people live there? How great would that be?"

"No, *people* don't live there, no." Note to self: visit Grandma.

After our ten-minute break and our first big convo as soon-to-be best buds, understudy rehearsal resumes and Jayne's first big number is up.

"Let's just have you sing it with Michael by the piano," Pete says. "Just like you did it at your final callback. Easy breezy." Pete's a pro. He knows that if stage fright can pop up once, it's likely to come back. He doesn't want to pressure her.

"Okay," Jayne says, making her way to the piano.

Michael, our musical director and conductor, plays the first few notes, and Jayne takes a breath and begins to sing.

I'm not exaggerating—I know I exaggerate a lot, but I'm not exaggerating this time. Hearing Jayne sing brings me back to the first time I heard Stella sing. It gives me the chills. The hairs on the back of my neck stand up as straight as a von Trapp kid post-whistle—well, the hair all over me, actually; I'm covered in it. It's a moment I'll never forget for as long as I live.

I'll admit it, Amanda has a great voice. She does. It's a fact. It's powerful and it's reliable; even if she didn't have a microphone, the people in the last row could hear her. Maya's voice is a bit more beautiful than Amanda's, albeit slightly less powerful. But she's a much better actress than Amanda—in my humble opinion.

But Jayne? Well, her talent surpasses theirs by a mile. When she sings, she makes us feel it. She makes us understand what she's singing about. It's not just vocal skill and it's not just acting skill; it's the perfect combination of both, topped off with a little extra something. It's . . .

You know those people who just have "it"? I'm not just talking about show business—although, it's clearly my main interest, I'll give you that.

You know the type: the kid who scores a dozen goals in a soccer game without breaking a sweat; the mom who throws together a five-cheese mac 'n' cheese from scratch on a Wednesday without even glimpsing at a recipe; your friend who can solve super complicated math problems in her head in under six seconds? They do what they do and they make it look easy. They make you wish that you could do it, too. To quote Ms. Lady Gaga (who needs to get to Broadway ASAP, btdubs), "They were born this way."

Well, my new friend Jayne? She's one of those people. She's got *it*.

When the song finishes, no one says anything for a solid thirty seconds. They just stand there. Some have their mouths open, some have tears in their eyes, everyone looks some version of shocked. That *that* much soul and heart could come out of a tiny girl like Jayne is . . . magic.

Maya is the first to speak. To quote my mother, "Maya's a good egg."

"Well, Jayne," Maya says, taking hold of her hand, "it's nice to know I'm leaving things in your very capable hands."

With that, everyone starts to clap, and relief floods Jayne's face.

"Thanks," she says simply. "It sure is a fun song."

"Even more fun with the dance," Maya adds.

"Let's get Jayne going with that, okay, Susie?" Pete directs.

"Absolutely," Susie says, striding toward center stage. Susie, like H.H., has legs for days. "Everyone! Let's take it from the top of the number. We'll run it once with Maya and then start teaching it to Jayne."

Sometimes, during understudy rehearsal, I'll help Pete call out a line if someone forgets theirs. Or I'll hop up onto the piano and turn pages while Michael plays. Sometimes I'll rehearse all of the Amanda role in the wings while Maya rehearses, because unlike Amanda, Maya doesn't mind.

But today, I just watch.

I watch my new friend "nail it," as Chris would say. Watch her rehearse to live her dream.

I watch my theatre family fall into splits and do double pirouettes, hit high notes with ease. Watch them work hard at the best job in the whole wide world.

And in that moment, in the cool stillness of the empty house, I wish on one of the painted stars on our sparkling ceiling, harder than I've ever wished for anything in my whole entire life.

Please let that be me one day. Please let me find a way. Please let me be the first mouse to perform on Broadway.

My moment.

My magic.

My miracle.

Let me be the first. But far from the last.

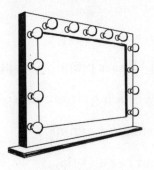

CHAPTER
SEVEN

S O," HEATHER HUFFMAN SAYS, PLACING ME ON the newly fluffed plush towel on her dressing room counter, "how's the new girl? How was today's understudy rehearsal? Tell me everything." I've just arrived to help with her usual preshow routine. Eyelashes, eyeliner, reassuring her that her mirror actually *is* lying to her. "I hear she's quite the little talent."

"She's fantastic," I say. "And so nice."

"Well, that's good to hear," H.H. says. "See? You were worried for nothing."

"It's like you always say, 'Worrying is natural and normal but serves no purpose,'" I quote.

"Precisely," H.H. says proudly. "Happy to know some of my sage wisdom is being absorbed, Tiny. Might as well learn from my mistakes, hmmm?"

I nod and hand her a Q-tip.

"You know, I made my Broadway debut as an understudy," Jodie Howard says. "And a *replacement*, God help me." Jodie is perched on the stool next to Heather Huffman, aggressively tweezing her eyebrows. "No opening night, and I barely got to perform. I've never been an understudy again. That's something you should only do once, if you can help it."

"Why?" I ask. Needless to say, I'd be an understudy in a minute. I'd be a rock if it meant performing on Broadway.

"Do it more than once, and that's how people see you. You'll be an understudy forever," Jodie says. "And it's emotionally draining, not knowing when you'll go on, *if* you'll go on. And once you go on. . . . Well, it's tough going back to the way things were before."

"I understudied a very famous actress," H.H. begins.

"You mean?" And Jodie pulls back her face to make herself look like Cruella de Vil, the cartoon version.

"Yes. *Her*. Only she didn't look like that back then. I was better in the role than she was and everyone knew it, but it didn't matter because she was famous," H.H. says, lining her lips. "*Awful*. Never again."

"I'd be an understudy in a minute," I say. "I'd be a rock if it meant being on Broadway." I said it to you, so I may as well say it to them, right?

H.H. and Jodie look at each other and then at me. It's the kind of look my mother gives me when she tucks me in at night. When she asks me what I'll dream about, and I always say, "Being on Broadway, Mom." It's a sadness, mixed with a desire to fix things, mixed with a whole lot of love.

"I know, Tiny," H.H. says.

"We shouldn't complain," Jodie adds. "That was highly inconsiderate of us."

"It's okay," I say, meaning it. "I like hearing your stories."

"Still," H.H. says. "Stories are one thing; complaints are another."

"Yes, yes, enough *kvetching*, as my ex-mother-in-law would say," Jodie barks.

"Kvetching?" I ask. Jodie's always coming up with words I've never heard of.

"It's Yiddish for complaining," Jodie says.

"Like *Fiddler*?" I ask.

And H.H. looks at me with such love, my heart could burst. "Yes, Tiny. Like *Fiddler*. Our little musical theatre expert never misses a beat."

"A theatre encyclopedia. You'd win big on Broadway *Jeopardy!*, and you'd share your money with us," Jodie says with a wink.

"Do you think it could ever happen?" I ask, doing my best not to tear up.

"What, darling?" Jodie asks. "*Jeopardy!*?"

"No. Me. On Broadway," I say. A mouse, on Broadway. A nonhuman, on Broadway.

"Well," H.H. says, scooping me up and holding me in her palms. "I've seen a lot in my lifetime. I, of course, won't tell you the exact, or approximate, length of that lifetime—"

"Neither will I, of course," Jodie adds.

"But. I've seen a lot. And a lot I never imagined. Good and bad. Medicines to help terrible diseases, changes to laws, a president or two I never expected to see. Multiple revivals of *The Glass Menagerie*." She rolls her eyes at that one.

"So, my dear Tiny, I certainly hope it happens. Because everyone—no matter the size or species—deserves to live their dream."

"I concur vehemently." Jodie nods in agreement.

"And in the meantime," H.H. says, placing me in front of her mirror. "You make believe."

She turns off the overhead dressing room lights and

turns on the mirror's lights instead.

"Feel that? That bright, blinding intensity? That feeling of being alone, but knowing there's so much out in front of you?"

"Yes," I say. I do. And it's magical.

"That's what stepping out onstage feels like," H.H. says.

I close my eyes and feel the lights bleeding through my eyelids. So strong and so bright, yet so comforting.

"Pretty fantastic, right?" Jodie says knowingly. "It never gets old."

"It feels like home," I say.

I keep my eyes closed, imagining the sound of the orchestra, the audience, the applause.

My daydream is swiftly interrupted by the sound of sniffles, and loud nose-blowing. I open my eyes to find H.H. and Jodie with tears in their eyes to match the ones in mine.

"Oh, sweet girl," H.H. says. "We love you so."

"I love you, ladies," I say. And I do. I really do. Friendship knows no age, size, or species, I suppose.

"Well," Jodie Howard says, with a good blow of her nose, "if a miracle can happen anywhere, it can happen in the theatre."

"I hope you're right," I say.

"Lucky for you," H.H. says, delicately tapping a folded tissue against her lower lash line, "my friend Jodie Howard is always right."

CHAPTER
EIGHT

I JUST DON'T UNDERSTAND WHY THEY *BOTH* HAVE TO be here," an all-too-familiar voice whines.

Guess who? If you guessed Amanda, you are correct, dear reader.

"They have to be here because it's their job," Milly says. Milly is trying to stay as calm as she can, but I can sense she's had it up to here with Amanda and her attitude. Out of everyone, Milly's got to be the most frustrated with this whole Amanda-rules-the-world thing.

"Actually, it's *my* job, but whatever," Amanda grumbles.

I'm in the third-floor hallway with Maya and Jayne, but the dressing room door is open, so we're still part of this scene. The Shubert's dressing rooms are small, by the way, and this one is made even smaller by Amanda's attitude at full capacity.

Maya's got a *this again* look on her face, while Jayne is super solemn, like she's slowly realizing that sometimes dreams aren't what we hoped they'd be. Sometimes dreams come with terms and conditions. Sometimes dreams come with Amanda.

"Amanda. This is not up for discussion. Both girls will trail you during the show today, per Pete's request, and that's final." Go, Milly! If I weren't so afraid of physical retaliation from Amanda, I would cheer out loud. But Jayne's arrival has made Amanda even more frenzied and unreasonable than usual, and there's no telling what she might throw or break. I wouldn't put it past her to throw or break a theatre-loving mouse.

"Fine," Amanda says, applying far too much blush, per usual. She actually listens to what Pete says because he's the only one who can call our director and report bad behavior. You should have seen her with the director. She was an angel. Then the moment the director left New York to direct a movie in Los Angeles, Amanda flipped a switch and landed in demon territory. "But they can't *say* anything. I can't have them disrupting my show."

"I'm sure Jayne will be just as polite as Maya always is," Milly says, turning to Jayne and Maya. "Right, ladies?"

Maya and Jayne nod, like obedient robots.

Why is it that bullies always get their way? Honestly. It makes me mad.

"Bet mentioned something about needing measurements for Jayne," I say. Full disclosure: this is a total lie. With a lot of help from my mom, Bet is already done with Jayne's costumes. I just want to save my friends and get them away from Amanda for a while. "I'll take Jayne and Maya downstairs for a minute and be right back. Is that okay, Milly?"

"Of course," Milly says. "Thanks, Lulu."

"Measurements? Measurements for what?" Amanda demands.

"For costumes," I say. What else would Bet need measurements for? Cabinetry? Curtains? Cookies? I mean, really.

"She's getting her own costumes?" Amanda looks like she's going to explode. You know Veruca Salt from the *Willy Wonka and the Chocolate Factory* movie? The one who wants the goose that lays the golden egg? That's who Amanda's channeling right now. (If you don't know what I'm talking about, envision a human tea kettle whistling and steaming. And make sure to watch the movie at some point because it's great.) "Why on earth does she need her own costumes?"

"Because she's *smaller* than we are, Amanda," Maya says, shedding her robotic stare in exchange for an *enough is enough* glare. I'm so proud I could whistle. (But I won't.)

"Oh, I'm *sorry*, I thought Milly had just instructed

you not to speak to me, *Maya*. Or are you so busy with your new friend plain Jayne that you didn't hear her?" Amanda's up on her feet now, inching toward Maya, Jayne, and me like she's some sort of large feline and we're . . . well . . . mice.

"Actually, what Milly said is that we'd be polite. I'm being perfectly polite. And Jayne hasn't said a word since she's gotten here," Maya replies.

It's true. The talkative Jayne from this afternoon's understudy rehearsal became silent Jayne the moment Amanda entered the building. To be fair, Maya and I had warned Jayne of Amanda's flair for the dramatic and fondness for aggression and downright meanness, so she was probably in self-preservation mode.

"Girls, please. Let's be civil," Milly warns.

Amanda huffs so hard I'm surprised she doesn't blow all the costumes off their racks.

Obviously, I'm finding Amanda's behavior absolutely ridiculous, but I can't help but think about what she just said. *Your new friend plain Jayne.* Not the "plain Jayne" part—that was just plain mean. No, I'm thinking more about the "new friend" part.

My mother is always telling me to put myself in someone else's shoes to better understand them. Could it be possible that Amanda is jealous—or is it envious? I'll have to check with H.H. for clarification—about our new friendship with Jayne? Come to think of it, Amanda doesn't have any real friends at the theatre. I mean, it makes sense. She's not very nice; why would anyone want to be friends with her? But maybe she puts up this mean front because she's really super insecure and is worried no one will like her? Lucy Louise, unlicensed therapist, at your service, I know. But think about it. You know kids like Amanda. Did it ever occur to you that maybe they act the way they do because underneath it all they're just plain scared?

"You know what, Maya," Amanda snaps, "I have had just about enough of you. Get out! You're no longer allowed in my dressing room."

Wow. Okay. Let's just put my psychological analysis on the back burner for a minute while we deal with this.

"Amanda, this is their dressing room, too. Please, calm down," Milly says.

"Oh, I'm perfectly calm. I just don't appreciate being spoken to in such a rude manner," Amanda says, hands on hips. "If you'll excuse me, I need to warm up my voice. *I* have a show tonight." And she slams the door, leaving all four of us in the hallway. Shut out and shut down.

"Yikes," Jayne says, as if her ability to produce words is directly linked to Amanda's presence.

"Let's give her a few minutes alone to cool off and go take a field trip to the wardrobe room, okay?" Milly says. "And please don't worry, Maya. I don't care what Amanda says; as long as your name's still on that dressing room door, you'll spend as much time in there as you like."

"That's the thing," Maya says, "I don't even like it in there anymore. I'd rather spend my last few days in the theatre somewhere else." Milly puts her arm around Maya's shoulders, and they start down the stairs.

Jayne pops me into her pocket—she's wearing a really cute purple romper with comfy front pockets—and says, "Should I be worried, Lulu?"

"No," I say, choosing to tell a little white lie for the sake of my new friend. "She's harmless."

"I don't know about that," Jayne says. "But I do know one thing for sure."

"What's that?" I ask.

"When I imagined my Broadway debut, I didn't imagine an Amanda to go along with it."

Of course, I want to remind her that at least she's employed on Broadway, regardless of Amanda. At least she's getting a shot. But I know this moment isn't about me and my lack of opportunity, so I just say, "Yeah. I get that."

From the second-floor landing, Milly calls, "Coming, girls?" and we start down the stairs after her, Jayne deep in thought, me deep in her pocket.

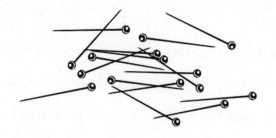

CHAPTER
NINE

ELL, HELLO, LADIES," BET SAYS. SHE'S ironing a dress shirt—what looks to be the final of a dozen or so, judging by the line of crisp shirts hanging next to her. The room smells warm and clean, like fabric softener and sunshine. "Isn't this a lovely surprise? I don't normally see you this close to Places."

"We came down to get away from Amanda," Maya says matter-of-factly. Less than two weeks left in the show and suddenly she's found her voice in a very big way.

"I see. Well, you're more than welcome to take refuge here. Mind the floor for pins, though," Bet says. "We had a spill earlier."

"That Chris is a dear, but he's incredibly clumsy," a very familiar voice says. Out from behind a cabinet pops my mother, carrying a pile of a dozen pins (like humans carry chopped wood). The pins are about half as tall as she is, but not too heavy. Nothing's too heavy for my mother.

"He was in here earlier, telling a story, and he's just so animated. He knocked over a brand-new box," Mom says, dropping the pins in the container Bet left on the floor for her.

Mom turns to my friends. "You must be Jayne."

"Yes, ma'am," Jayne says.

"Lucy Louise, your manners to match," my mother says.

This is one of my mother's signature sayings: "Your manners to match." If your parents happen to read this book, don't be surprised if they start saying it, too. While it pains me to admit, it's catchy.

"Mom, this is Jayne. Jayne, this is my mom."

"It's a pleasure to meet you," Jayne says, with a tiny curtsy.

"Likewise," my mom replies, clearly impressed by the poise of this tiny human. "Maya, Milly, I hope my daughter is behaving herself."

"Mom!" I say, being wary not to wander into a whine. In case you couldn't guess, my mother's not big on whining.

"She's a delight," Milly says. "A welcome and integral member of our company."

"She's the only reason I survived ten months with Amanda," Maya says.

"Oh, yes, I've heard all about that," Mom says, her expression shifting a bit. "I'm glad my daughter could be of assistance."

"She's a great friend," Jayne says, with all the sincerity in the world.

My mother looks at me and smiles. "Well, isn't that a kind thing to say, Jayne. It makes me proud to know I've raised a good friend."

"Five Minutes, this is your Five-Minute call. Five Minutes, please." Today's show is being called by Ricardo. (Pete's daughter has a concert at school that he couldn't miss.) Ricardo's voice sounds like Cool Ranch salad dressing.

"Before you girls head off, I've got something to show you," Bet says, leading us over to the far corner of the wardrobe room and revealing a rolling rack of sparkling new tiny costumes.

"Are those . . . ?" Jayne can barely get the words out.

"Your costumes? Yes, they are," Bet says.

They're beautiful. They're breathtaking. I'm envious. Let's continue.

I look to Maya. She's trying to be kind and not ruin Jayne's moment, but I can see she's struggling. She's . . . jealous, I guess? Technically, something's being taken away from her, so, yes. I think it's jealousy and not envy. I'll check with H.H.

Maya never had her own costumes—aside from

undergarments and shoes, of course—because she and Amanda were exactly the same size when rehearsals started. She barely got to perform and she had to share costumes with a gal whose first word was most likely "Mine!" It was a Broadway debut, sure, but I'm certain it wasn't the one she dreamed of all her life. It was a half debut at best. I hope next time, whether it's in two years or twenty, Maya returns to Broadway in a role of her own. She deserves it.

"Aren't they beautiful?" Maya says. She's such a good sport. "The sparkly blue has always been my favorite. What do you think, Jayne?"

Jayne walks over to the rack, like she's admiring a piece of art at a museum. But she doesn't touch it. (From what I hear, touching anything at museums is a big no-no.)

"May I?" she asks.

"Of course," Bet says. "They're yours."

Jayne runs her hand across the row, delicately skimming each costume. "In community theatre, we always had old costumes," she says. "Stinky and old."

This isn't the first time I've heard this about other theatres. They use old costumes that have already been worn on Broadway and on national tours. Inevitably stinky and worn out, I'm sure, but better than nothing.

"Here on Broadway, we start from scratch," my mother says. "Isn't that right, Lucy Louise?"

"Yep," I say. "Only the best here on Broadway."

I glance at my mom and she has the same look in her eyes as our director did when she read our show's rave review in the *New York Times*—a mix of pride, love, and hope.

"You're the best thing I ever made," my mother once told me. Then she followed it with, "Don't tell your brothers."

And I know she knows what I'm thinking. Isn't it amazing that parents always know what we're thinking? It's like the moment we were born their love for us gave them magical powers.

I'm thinking how much I want a sparkly blue dress in my size. A sparkly blue, and a puffy pink, and a vanilla velvet. Patent leather tap shoes and soft, satin slippers. I want it all.

I know, I know, "I want, I want." It's so unattractive. But I'm not a gal who asks for much. I don't want new cushioning for my nest; I love sleeping on the foam padding that once protected H.H.'s holiday candle in its schmancy box. I don't want to be taller; I don't want more friends. I don't even want to be human. I really like who and what I am.

I have one desire, one wish, one thing I truly, truly want—the dresses are just a part of that thing. I want to be on Broadway.

Is that so much to ask?

You know what? It is a lot to ask. There are thousands of people in New York City alone who dream of being on Broadway, and who work hard every day to try to make it happen. And even if they work as hard as they possibly can, they may not "make it." I'm not great with math, but I'd guess that the odds of a human making it to Broadway are way worse than the odds of a human being pooped on by a New York City pigeon.

The thing that frustrates me is that I don't even have a chance at trying out. What do they say in baseball? You can't hit a home run if you never get off the bench? (Shout-out to my dad and his crew guy friends Dan and Artie who stand by their New York Mets, even though they don't win very often.)

I'm not even on the bench. I'm under it.

CHAPTER
TEN

A ND THEN YOU SHAKE YOUR SHOULDERS LIKE this," Maya says, shimmying her shoulders like she's wearing bells and wants them to ring in rhythm. She and I are teaching Jayne our overture dance.

"This is fun!" Jayne says, following along as if she's done the dance all her life.

"Isn't she just the cutest," I hear Harper, one of the chorus girls, say to Agnes, another chorus girl. "She's pint-sized."

"Pint-sized and talented," Agnes says. "You should have seen her in understudy rehearsal. Un. Real."

Amanda groans loudly and stomps across the stage, passing us. "Milly. I need you."

"Come dance with us first!" Milly calls.

"Now."

Milly looks to us and shrugs, following Amanda offstage left. Luckily, I have spectacular hearing—it's a mouse thing—so I don't even have to leave my dance spot to hear their conversation.

"I don't want her here," Amanda says.

"Who?" Milly asks.

"Her. *Jayne.*"

"I understand that, Amanda," Milly says, "but you really don't have a choice in the matter."

"They're always leaving me out!" Amanda blurts.

"Is that what this is about?" Milly asks, softening. "You feel left out?"

"What? No. I never said that," Amanda says. Um . . . what? She literally just said that. "Everyone's *obsessed* with her. It's ridiculous. *I'm* the star."

"Yes, you are. And it wouldn't hurt you to start behaving like one."

Amanda glares at Milly. If her eyes were laser beams, Milly would be fried.

"And *you* are a *wannabe* actress who has to take care of kids because she doesn't have what it takes to be on Broadway."

Milly looks at Amanda with such hurt, it's possible her heart is actually aching. Then she scrunches her mouth up, sighs, and says, "That was an incredibly hurtful thing to say, Amanda. After bows, I expect an apology. For now, let's focus on our show."

"*My* show," Amanda says. "Not *yours*, not *Maya's*, not *Jayne's*, and certainly not *Lulu's*. Mine."

Amanda takes her place behind the upstage door, preparing for her entrance, smiling at the other actors as though she hasn't just spewed nastiness all over offstage left. (Not as much nastiness as the time she puked in a bucket offstage right, I'd like to remind her.)

The overture is about to finish up, and everyone "mouse hops" into the wings.

"Are you okay?" Maya asks. "What did Amanda say?"

"Nothing worth repeating," Milly says. "Let's just do our jobs, girls. That's what's important right now."

But there's no fooling us. Milly's light is out again, dimmer than I've ever seen it. Amanda managed to hit her where it hurt most. She hit her in her dream. I forget, sometimes. Milly dreams of being on Broadway, too. She didn't go to a fancy musical theatre conservatory because she wanted to take care of a bunch of kids. The job fell into her lap, she took it, and she's great at it. "I'd rather work in the theatre, one way or another," she told me once.

It's no wonder we get along so well. We're two peas in a wanna-be-on-Broadway pod.

"Are you sure, Milly?" Jayne asks.

"Yes. I'm sure," Milly says, literally shaking it off, with a sigh and a smile. "Now. Take a look at where Amanda is. That's your opening spot. Got it?"

"Got it," Jayne says.

"And after the first number, she'll exit stage right, go downstairs to the hair room where Jeremiah will change her wig, then cross under the stage to get back up to the dressing room," Maya says.

"Let's go take a reverse-walk under there so you can see how long it takes," Milly says, leading us toward the stage left stairwell.

And then I see something they don't. I see Stella.

She's spent the overture dance in the quick-change booth, not in her usual spot on the other side of the stage.

We lock eyes.

That "private" conversation between Amanda and Milly? Stella heard every word.

CHAPTER
ELEVEN

G IRLS, WOULD YOU ALL JOIN ME IN MY DRESS-
ing room for a moment?" Stella says.

Holy cannoli. It's after the show, and I can't believe what's happening. We all survived tonight's show, despite Amanda's best efforts to pulverize us with evil-eye glares, and we're all on our way downstairs to go home.

Amanda's, Maya's, and Jayne's parents are outside waiting in Shubert Alley to take them home. It's a union (and probably federal?) rule that any performer under the age of sixteen cannot be unchaperoned in the theatre. Hence, Milly. The girls' parents hand them off to Milly before the show, and she hands them back afterward. Amanda's mother had a tendency to "overstay her welcome" backstage when the show first opened, so Pete made an unofficial rule: no parents backstage unless previous permission is granted.

Rules, tools, schmools. What's important in this very moment is: Stella is asking us to join her in her dressing room! To quote *Annie*, "Could someone pinch me, please?"

"Of course, Stella," Amanda says, turning on her best fake smile. Her smile is so saccharine I'm surprised her teeth don't fall out.

"Wonderful," Stella says. We follow her in, and the room smells as delightfully fragrant as ever—heavy on the lilac today—and there's her assistant Trish typing away on her phone, and Chris putting away the last of Stella's costumes.

"Hey, y'all, it's a par-tay," Chris practically sings. "Who brought the champagne?"

"Oh, *Christopher*, you know we can't drink *alcohol*," Amanda says, sounding like some sort of crazy . . . well, to be honest, she sounds like her crazy mother.

"*Christopher* was just *joking*, boo," Chris says to Amanda, grabbing a pair of shoes that clearly need the polishing expertise of my mom's tiny feet. "Night, ladies."

We all say our goodnights, Amanda's being the loudest. (Ick.) I catch Chris rolling his eyes so hard it's amazing they don't roll right out of his head.

"I'll go tell the fans you'll be a few minutes," Trish says, leaving the room. On a normal night, there are at least a hundred fans waiting in Shubert Alley for Stella, and she signs autographs for every single one. She feels it's part of her job and she's happy to do it. It's her "duty" as a leading lady with her name above the title to respect the fans and show gratitude to them for being loyal to her. (Side note: having her name above the title on the marquee and on posters and such means that if Stella isn't at a performance, theatregoers can return their tickets. It's a lot of pressure. On her, and on her understudy.)

Not every star greets the fans after a show, you know. For starters, some are just too tired post-show, and I guess that's understandable. Being well rested vocally and physically so they're able to perform is top priority. Then there are others who never sign autographs, and frankly, that just isn't cool in my book. I won't name names, but I happen to know of at least a dozen Broadway stars who often sneak out their theatre's back exits because they "don't want to deal with the fans." How do I know this, you ask? Well, let's just say I've got family in Broadway basements, ceilings, and walls, with big mouths and even bigger ears.

"Sit down, girls, sit down," Stella says, pointing to her super comfy couch. (Not that I've ever sat on it; I'm just guessing, by the look of it.)

"Thanks," Milly says, and we all sit. And it's comfy. Super comfy. Wow. It's like floating on a cloud. Not literally, figuratively. You know what I mean. Wow.

It reminds me of the time the Hooligans had the genius idea of using Jet-Puffed Marshmallows as living room chairs. Delightful until they got sticky, and our friends the Ants showed up. That family gets around, I'll tell ya. They'd come to the opening of an envelope full of cake crumbs.

This is an actual scene I observed between the Hooligans, the Ants, and, eventually, my mother:

THE SETTING: *Our family living room*

THE DAY: *Saturday*

THE TIME: *Ten minutes into Act Two, approximately 9:35 pm*

*The Hooligans—*WALT, MATTY, TIMMY, *and* BENJI*—each recline on a Jet-Puffed Marshmallow. They sigh, the comfort almost too good to be true.*

In march dozens of members of the Ant family. The Hooligans jump up, bits of marshmallow sticking to their hairy bodies.

WALT   Dudes. You can't be here!

TAD THE ANT   In case you haven't heard, Walt, this is

a free country, and my family and I can visit any

darn theatre we like.

MATTY   Come on, guys, our mom's gonna go nuts!

At the mention of the word "nuts" a few of the Ants
look around, expectantly.

TIMMY   We're not supposed to have parties!

TRAVIS THE ANT   We heard about the marshmallows.

NICK THE ANT   We came for the marshmallows.

KEVIN THE ANT   Jet-Puffed? The legends are true!

Enter our mom.

MOM   Would someone like to explain to me exactly

what is going on here?

WALT   Benji did it.

They all turn to BENJI, *who doesn't even bother to fight,*
hanging his head in defeat. . . .

End scene

Back to now in Stella's dressing room, Jayne is still not quite sure this is real life. Her eyes are even wider and bigger than usual, and they're flitting around the room taking this all in: the elegant bouquets of flowers, the photos of Stella with her famous friends, Stella's state-of-the-art humidifier from Switzerland. I mean, *I'm* finding the experience super bananas and I've known Stella for ten months already. Jayne's been here for a day. She's losing it, and rightfully so.

"What's up, Stella?" Amanda asks, like they're best friends or something. *Phony baloney.*

"Well," Stella says, easing into her oatmeal-colored linen dressing room chair, her mirror's lights dancing across her perfect, pimple-less face, "I know you're leaving us soon, Maya, and I just wanted to say what a pleasure it's been working with you."

"Thank you," Maya says, fighting back her now signature tears. "It's been a pleasure working with you, too."

"You bring such a nice energy to the company, and you're very talented. I'm sure you'll go far."

"I hope so," Maya says.

"And you, Jayne, I know you just joined us today, so I thought I'd take a moment to introduce myself."

Jayne looks to me for verification that this is actually happening, that she's not in a dream, or an alternate universe where Broadway stars casually speak to little girls on the regular. I smile and nod. This is real. I can't believe it, either, but it's real.

"Oh, I . . . I . . . ," Jayne manages.

"I hear you're quite the talent," Stella says.

"Oh, I . . . I . . ."

"She is," I say. "She nailed understudy rehearsal today."

"She did," Milly says. "She'll be ready in no time."

"You know, I started off as an understudy," Stella says, sipping her hot water with lemon and wildflower honey (from bees she raises at her country home upstate).

"Really?" Jayne says. Finally, more than a stutter. Go, Jayne!

"Yes, when I was fourteen. In a show with Elaine Stritch."

(Elaine Stritch is a show business legend. Get permission from a legal guardian, then Google her, immediately.)

"Wow," I say, as if I didn't already know. When the show moved in, Timmy managed to find a Stella James biography, so we clocked some brother-sister bonding time while also learning everything there is to know about Stella James.

"It's a tough job, as Maya well knows," Stella says, "but I'm sure you're up for the challenge, Jayne."

"Who did you understudy?" Milly asks.

"Darcy Monroe," Stella replies.

"Never heard of her," Amanda snips.

"No, you probably haven't," Stella says. "You see, this was many years ago, and Darcy hasn't done another Broadway show since."

"Why not?" Jayne asks.

"Well, I'm not sure of the exact reason, but I do know she burned a lot of bridges during our show," Stella says, settling into her story. "Really, whoever knows what's going on inside someone's head, but on the outside, Darcy was combative. She'd pick a fight with anyone and everyone. And the way she treated me? Well. It was unacceptable. It was hard on me, and it was hard for everyone else to watch, you know? I'm just glad I didn't let it break my spirit."

Amanda looks like she ate a big spoonful of spoiled yogurt right before she had to walk onstage at a beauty pageant. She's smiling, but her mouth is all smooshed up, her nose is wrinkled, and her eyes are bulging.

"Everything all right, dear?" Stella asks.

"I'm fine," Amanda says, realizing, I suppose, that what she's feeling on the inside has indeed revealed itself on the outside. She softens her face a bit and says, "I bet Darcy has worked. You just don't know about it."

Man, she's bold. If I didn't know any better, I'd think she was picking a fight. Don't pick a fight with Tony Award winner Stella James, girl. You won't win.

"I suppose that's true, Amanda," Stella says. "And I also suppose it's true that the way Darcy treated all of us—especially me—wasn't really about us. It was about her. For all I know, she was struggling with some issues of her own and she just took it out on the rest of us. Probably would have been wise for her to simply be honest, but honesty isn't always easy."

Amanda's face starts to curl up again, but she quickly snaps it back to basic. Then she says, "Maybe you just saw her the way you wanted to see her because you were her understudy and you were jealous."

Wow. Wow. *Wow.*

"Amanda . . . ," Milly warns. "Girls. Maybe it's time we let Stella head home."

"Probably best we all get home and get a good night's sleep," Stella says. "See you tomorrow."

We all say a handful of exaggerated goodnights in an effort to blow past the awkwardness and go to leave.

"Oh," Stella says, giggling a bit. "I just remembered something Elaine said to Darcy, all those years ago—when she could no longer stay silent and let Darcy get away with her appalling behavior."

And I swear to you on all that is true and dear to me—my family, this theatre, the von Trapp kids, real and fictional—Stella looks directly at Amanda and says, "It gets tiring being a smart a—"

I obviously can't finish the word. But[t] you get the gist.

CHAPTER
TWELVE

OVER THE NEXT WEEK, THE ENERGY BACK-stage is . . . cloudy. Fishy. In need of an air purifier—an expensive one. Amanda was thrown into a tizzy by what Stella said to her, even though we all did our best to convince her that it was just a funny Elaine Stritch story and nothing more. We're still trying to convince her—though we know *exactly* what Stella meant—and Amanda's not buying it.

"If I wasn't worried about being blacklisted, I'd report her to the union," Amanda says, tapping on her new *French* lip *beurre*. (*Beurre* is French for "butter." The fact that Amanda has a French *anything* makes me want to abandon my love of the language and take up Italian.) "But she's so powerful. She's with the number-three talent agency, you know."

Yes! We know! You mention it every livelong day! We also know that Amanda's dream (or is it her mother's dream?) is to sign with Stella's talent agency, so she can beat out Marlee Matlin and become the youngest winner of the Academy Award for Best Actress. Yeah, like *that* will ever happen. Go buy a lotto ticket while you're at it, girly.

"Milly. You should tell Pete. What she said borders on harassment."

"It was just a post-show conversation, Amanda," Milly says. "A show business story. An Elaine Stritch story. You love Elaine Stritch. She's a legend."

"As if. She couldn't really sing," Amanda says. Um . . . go tell that to Stephen Sondheim and the Carlyle Hotel, you loon. "And she wasn't even funny on *30 Rock*." Okay, now she's downright lying through her Invisalign-wearing teeth.

"Anyway, it was over a week ago. I think it's time to let it go," Milly says. For the record, Milly has said this every day for the last ten days. But you know Amanda. She doesn't let anything go. "Let's just talk about something else," Milly says.

"Fine," Amanda says, shifting gears. "Maya. Are you sad this is your last day here?"

Maya's eyes instantly water, and Jayne puts her tiny arm around Maya's shoulder. I'm so mad the hook in my tail almost straightens out.

"Amanda," Milly says. "Please be more considerate."

"You said to talk about something *else*. Everyone is making a big deal about her leaving; I suppose I should, too."

In truth, everyone *is* making a big deal about Maya's departure. The gals in the ensemble dressing room got her a little box of Angel Cards just like the ones they have. It's a wooden box of seventy or so little cards, with words like "wisdom," "hope," or "spontaneity" written on them, surrounded by curly, dreamy artwork. Before each show, the chorus girls each pick a card and the idea is that it's meant to inspire their performances and the rest of their day. Maya has always loved them. Now she has her own set to bring with her to her next show. Or to college—whichever comes first. Stella sent her a super fancy orchid plant from the super fancy florist on Fifty-First Street. Our company manager even let Maya pick the quote of the week for this week's pay stub. She picked, "I shall stay until the wind changes," from *Mary Poppins*, which made everyone ugly cry.

Yes, our company has done their best to brighten up Maya's remaining time in the theatre, but Amanda's doing her darndest to muck it all up. Not on my watch.

"Maya. Want to go up to the fly floor to say goodbye to Dan and Artie?" I ask.

"Yes!" she says. "May we, Milly?"

"I suppose so. But be back by Five Minutes to Places. And be careful."

"Great," Maya says. "You want to join, Jayne?"

"Sure!" Jayne says. "But what's the fly floor?"

"It's where a lot of the backstage magic happens," I say.

"Oh!" Jayne says. "Where is it?"

"Follow us," I say, scurrying up Maya's dress and into her hand. "It's just upstairs."

Okay. Full disclosure, I was totally scared the first time I went up to the fly floor. Walt and Matty love playing up there—it's where they go if it's snowing out and they can't play in the alley—and my dad likes to go up and watch Mets games with Dan and Artie, the crew guys who man the fly floor. But it's high up. High. Envision a super high balcony that goes all the way around the perimeter of the stage's ceiling, and that's the fly floor.

To get there, you've got to head two flights up from the girls' dressing room, then up a ladder on the side of a wall. It's only six rungs, but it goes straight up, so it's a little intimidating.

Once you've done it a few times, it's not so bad, but Jayne hasn't done it a few times. Jayne hasn't done it one time, and she's staring at it like it's the scariest thing on the planet. (Which I'm sure it's not. I mean, have you heard about *sharks*? How can those even be real?!)

"Don't worry," Maya says. "It's easy. Like the jungle gym at school."

"I broke my wrist on the jungle gym at school," Jayne says.

"Okay, bad example," Maya says, plopping me in her pocket so she can climb with both hands.

"Who's being loud?" a New York accent booms. It's Dan. He was just as scary as the ladder when I first met him. Now he's my favorite. My favorite crew guy, that is. (P.S. I'm pretty sure he has a crush on H.H., and, frankly, she could do worse.)

"It's just us, Dan," I say, popping my head out of Maya's pocket.

"I'm here to say goodbye," Maya says.

"I hate goodbyes," he says, peering down at us. "Who's this?"

"This is Jayne. My replacement," Maya says. "Don't worry. She's great."

"Nice to meet you, Jayne. Come on up, check out the view."

"I . . . I . . . I don't think I can," Jayne says, inching away from the ladder.

"It's easy," Maya says again, stepping on the first rung.

"I . . . I . . . don't think so," Jayne stutters. She's up against the opposite wall now, frozen solid like she was the first time I met her. I know what I have to do.

"Let me down, Maya," I say. She sets me down and I scurry over to Jayne faster than you can say "That new show starring Nathan Lane? It's sold out."

"What's up?" I ask, even though I already know. Sometimes it's good to let someone tell you something in their own time and words.

"I fell. On the jungle gym. What if I fall, and I . . ." Jayne stops, her face frozen like she's envisioning the worst thing in the whole entire world.

"And you what?" I ask, even though I know. I know what the worst thing in the whole entire world is to my friend Jayne, because it would be the worst thing to me, too.

"What if I fall and I ruin my Broadway debut? What if I'm out before I even—"

"Get up to the plate?" I reply. Whoa. Another baseball reference? Where the heck did that come from? Somewhere in this building, my father has never been so proud.

"Yeah," she says, brightening a little. "You like baseball?"

"I don't. But my family does. So do Dan and Artie up there," I point.

"I love baseball. Weird for a girl, I know," she says.

"Nothing is weird for anyone," Dan yells down.

"Anyone who tells you otherwise, you tell them to take a long walk off a short pier."

"Okay." Jayne snorts out a tiny giggle. "Dan."

"So. You want to give it a try?" Maya asks.

"I . . . I don't know," Jayne says.

I look up at her with the same confidence I did during her first bout of stage fright. "How about I go first?" I say.

She nods, and I scurry over to the ladder, weaving my way up each rung until I'm at the top, right at Dan's feet, looking down at Jayne.

"If I can do it, you can do it," I say.

Jayne takes a deep breath, walks over, and, slowly but surely, climbs her way to the top.

CHAPTER
THIRTEEN

W "ow."

For the record, *wow* doesn't begin to cover it, but it's all Jayne's got for now. We're up on the fly floor, surrounded by ropes and pulleys, looking down through the curtains and lights onto the stage, a stage that's been here since 1913. A stage that's seen hits and flops, thousands of Broadway debuts and hundreds of return engagements. A stage where, right now, our cast members are beginning to gather for their preshow warm-ups and, soon, our overture dance.

Through the curtain, we can hear the gentle murmur of the audience arriving and settling into their seats—hopefully turning off their cell phones and unwrapping any noisy candies. Down in the orchestra pit, the musicians are tuning their instruments; it's an improvised cacophony of scales—bright bursts from the horns, fluttery warbles from the strings—and yet it somehow all comes together beautifully to make perfect, erratic sense.

It's all below us, and we're up where it feels like the top of the world. From up here, everyone looks just as small as I am. From up here, I don't feel small at all.

Let me clarify. We're not in any real danger. This is by no means a narrow space. There's room enough for a couch, a TV, and a minifridge—all supplied by Dan and Artie, of course. From what I hear, it's bigger than most New York City apartments. It's not narrow; it's just high. And we're completely surrounded by sturdy, metal railings, so it's perfectly safe.

"Amazing, right?" Maya says, taking it all in for the last time.

"It's incredible," Jayne says.

"Someday when you're more settled, come up during the show and I'll let you move a set piece or two," Artie says. He's parked in front of his TV watching the Giants game. (It's winter, so it's time for football, not baseball. Sports, blah, blah, blah, sports.)

"Really? Isn't it all super heavy?" Jayne asks.

"Some of it's heavy. Some of it's just buttons," Artie says.

"You know not to whistle, right, kid?" Dan asks, his scratchy, bold voice booming out over the stage.

"What do you mean?" Jayne asks.

"Before our time, the stage crew used to communicate by whistling. So, you whistle, you risk a curtain nailing you on your noggin." (You already know this, but it's the first Jayne's hearing of it, so I figured it was worth a second mention.)

"It's a superstition," I say. "We also never say 'good luck,'" I whisper.

"That I knew," Jayne says.

"Or the M-word Shakespeare play. That's a big no-no," Dan says.

"The M-word?"

"Ask someone when you're not in a theatre," Dan says. (It's *Macbeth*. I'm pretty sure writing it isn't bad luck. But saying it inside the theatre will apparently cause disaster, according to the superstition, aka "the Scottish curse.")

I look over and see Maya peering down over the stage, with such a look on her face.

"It sure is pretty," she says.

"It sure is," I say.

"Most kids never even set foot in a theatre like this," Maya says. "Let alone every day for ten months. For money."

"Yeah," I say.

"I guess I should feel lucky I even had two shows out there, right?" she says, looking at me.

Um, *yes*, I want to say. *Très* lucky. But I know if I were her, I'd feel the same way. Sure, now I just want the chance; I want to know it's even a possibility. But imagine giving *me* two performances on Broadway and then no more after that. I'd be thankful, but I'd still want more. That's love, I guess. You can never get enough of your true love. It's like the Hooligans with a bucket of kettle corn. One kernel is never enough.

"I wish you could have had more performances," I say. "Amanda wasn't nice about it."

"I can't really blame her," Maya says. "If it were my role, I wouldn't want to miss a show, either."

This is true, but missing a few more performances wouldn't have hurt her. Or any of us, for that matter. A day off for Amanda is a day off for all.

"I hope I get to go on," Jayne says dreamily, quickly catching herself. "Sorry. I didn't mean to be inconsiderate."

"Not at all," Maya says. "I wish you my two performances, and many more."

"Thanks," Jayne says.

"And I hope you get your wish, too, Lulu," Maya says.

"What's your wish, Lulu?" Jayne asks. And I realize I've never mentioned it to her. This whole time I've been so focused on Jayne, I never really took the time to tell her anything about myself.

"Oh. Well. It's to perform. On Broadway. Seems like an easy ask since I live in a Broadway theatre and have basically had free master classes since birth and all, but it's not. It's . . . complicated."

"Oh," Jayne says. People always seem to say "oh" when they're not quite sure what else to say.

"No dream is too big, no dreamer too small," Artie says.

Really, Artie? Just when you think he's just this Santa look-alike who watches sports all day and moves scenery in the evenings, he comes out with something like that.

"How eloquent," Dan says. "My pal Shakespeare over here."

"What can I say? It just came to me," Artie says. "I believe in miracles." (Maybe he *is* Santa Claus?!)

"Anything can happen, Lulu," Maya says. "And in the meantime, half the fun is dreaming about it."

"That's true!" Jayne says supportively. "If I can do it, you can do it, right?"

"Right," I say, only half believing it. I'm getting to the point where the hope hurts too much.

"Five Minutes, this is your Five-Minute call. Five Minutes, please," Pete's voice pipes out of the speaker next to Artie.

"Well, I guess this is it," Maya says. "My last Five-Minute call."

"May there be many more Five-Minute calls in your future," Artie says.

"You're on a roll today, Shakespeare," Dan says. "Don't be a stranger, kid, ya hear?"

"I won't," Maya says. "We'd better go. We promised Milly." She takes one last look at the stage down below, wipes a tear from her cheek, and heads to the ladder.

"By the way," I say to Maya, "while Amanda's onstage

tonight there's something we need to do."

"What is it?" she asks.

"It's a surprise," I say.

"Come on, you guys! We'll be late for the overture dance!" Jayne says, stepping back down the ladder like a pro.

"After Amanda's first entrance, we all will meet up in the dressing room," I say.

"Okay," Maya says, shooting me a suspicious yet excited glance. She leans down, opens her palms, I hop into her hands, and we all hurry downstairs to the stage for Maya's final overture dance.

CHAPTER
FOURTEEN

B Y THE TIME AMANDA'S FIRST NUMBER BEGINS, Maya, Milly, Jayne, and I have reconvened in the dressing room.

"What is this all about?" Maya asks.

"Tradition," I say. "Well, superstition." I'm on top of the dressing room counter holding a penny. My arms are shaking because copper is *très* heavy, but so help me, I will keep holding this penny and create a memorable moment for all of us. Thank goodness this tradition doesn't involve a nickel or a quarter. "Before a performer leaves the theatre for the last time, they must tape a penny under their dressing room counter."

"What for?" Maya asks.

"To ensure you'll be back in another show someday," Milly says.

"For that, I'll tape a hundred pennies," Maya says, taking the penny from me and crawling under the counter. Phew, that's a relief. I whip my arms around a few times to make sure they don't cramp up. I really need to work on my upper body strength.

"Here," Jayne says, crouching down to hand Maya a piece of tape. "Wait. Better make it two pieces, so it lasts."

I knock a Sharpie off the counter—the silver kind the actors use to autograph Playbills—scurry down the leg of the counter, pick up the Sharpie, and slowly stride over to Maya. Awkward, yes, but not as heavy as the penny.

"Lulu, let me get that," Milly says. "That Sharpie is taller than you are."

"I've got it," I say.

"You never cease to amaze me," Milly says.

"What's that Shakespeare line?" Maya asks. "'Though she be but little . . . ?'"

"She is fierce!" Jayne says. "My mom got me a pencil case with that line on it."

"I think it's safe to say that verse applies to everyone in this room," Milly says.

"Okay, Maya," I say. "Now that you've taped the penny under the counter, all you have to do is sign your name and date it."

"The penny?" Jayne asks.

"The counter," Milly says.

"Oh," Jayne giggles. "That makes more sense."

Maya Cogan. Was here. A lot, she writes. *And she loved it*, she adds, dating it and adding a heart around the whole thing.

"What's going on?"

We were all so caught up in Maya's moment that we didn't realize Amanda's number was over.

"Oh, hey, Amanda, we were just . . . ," Maya starts.

"Maya was taping a penny under the dressing room counter," Milly says. Notice, she doesn't say *her* dressing room counter or *your* dressing room counter. A general *the* will hopefully keep the peace.

"And signing her name," Jayne adds matter-of-factly. Little, but fierce, indeed!

"Why?!" Amanda counters.

"It's a theatre tradition," I say firmly.

Amanda takes a moment, like she's debating her next move, then says, "Well, if it's tradition, I guess that's all right."

Maya looks at me as if to say, "Are we dreaming?" but before we can even say thank you to Amanda for being thoughtful, she says, "Move, Jayne. I need to change my clothes for the next scene." Amanda aggressively removes her shoes, and we all make room, lest we be injured by a flying tap shoe.

CHAPTER
FIFTEEN

I T'S TUESDAY, THE DAY AFTER OUR DAY OFF, AND everything's the same as last week except Maya's gone. She's gone from the sign-in sheet, her name plaque no longer hangs on the dressing room door or on the board in the lobby, even her show shoes and undergarments aren't in their usual spots. The photos that hung on her dressing room mirror, her dance clothes for understudy rehearsals, the scarf she was knitting to keep busy during the show—all gone.

Bet let her keep all four pairs of her show shoes, which Maya was very excited about. "Hopefully my feet don't grow so I can wear the sparkly ones to my friend

Cassie's bat mitzvah in the fall," she'd said. The whole cast, including Maya and the other understudies, went to the Tony Awards last June, so I can't imagine a bat mitzvah will compare, but who knows. Apparently they're a really big deal.

Yes, our dear Maya is back to normal life in New Jersey, and Jayne has taken her place. I liked it better when they were both here, but if Maya has to be gone, I'm glad it's Jayne who's taking over. The whole company has been very welcoming to Jayne. H.H. and Jodie seem especially fond of her. And I'm not one bit jealous. There is plenty of H.H. and Jodie Howard attention to go around.

Jayne's with me in H.H.'s and Jodie's dressing room to witness my preshow routine with H.H. I doubt she'll tag along all the time, but if she does, that's okay by me.

"Here, honey," H.H. says, handing Jayne a brand-new package of false eyelashes. "For luck."

"Thank you," Jayne says, holding them delicately, like they're the most precious gift she's ever received.

"You need help putting them on, you just ask Lulu. She's an expert," H.H. says.

"If I ever get to wear them, I will," Jayne says.

"*When* you wear them," H.H. scolds. "Positive affirmation, young lady."

"Sorry," Jayne says. *"When."*

"Has anyone ever told you, you resemble a young Judy Garland?" Jodie Howard asks loudly, brushing on her eye shadow in a repetitive half-moon motion.

"No," Jayne says, grinning from ear to ear. Introduce me to a theatre gal who doesn't welcome a Judy Garland comparison and I'll collapse in disbelief.

"Well, you do," Jodie says, swirling her brush in her Merry Mauve shadow and continuing on to the other eye.

"Thanks," Jayne says. "I love *The Wizard of Oz*."

"Who doesn't?" Jodie practically yells, throwing out her arms for emphasis, her makeup brush flying across the room. "It's a masterpiece. First movie ever to be made in color. It was a very big deal. Not that I was there, of course. I'm not *that* old."

"Tell me, Jayne, how's the wicked witch of the dressing room downstairs treating you?" H.H. asks, giggling a bit at her quick-wittedness. Then she stops herself. "I'm sorry. That was in poor taste. I'm an adult. I should know better. Amanda. How is Amanda treating you?"

"Oh, fine," Jayne says.

"Not true," I say. "She's just as unfriendly to Jayne as she was to Maya. Maybe even more so."

"That's probably because you're small and fresh and new, and she's . . . well . . . blossoming," H.H. says.

"Blossoming?" Jayne asks.

"Puberty," Jodie says, retrieving her brush. "It happens to everyone, but that doesn't make it more bearable."

"My brother has a lot of pimples," Jayne says.

"Very common," Jodie says. "I was covered in them from ages twelve to fourteen."

"I've always had a flawless complexion," H.H. says, dreamily examining her pores in the mirror.

"You, though, you've got plenty of time," Jodie says. "How old are you? Nine?"

"Eleven," Jayne says.

"You look nine," Jodie says. "Anyone asks, you're nine. Got it?"

"Got it," Jayne replies.

"Height?"

"Four feet, four inches," Jayne says. You can always count on a show biz kid to know their measurements.

"Four feet, four inches. Lordy. I think I was *born* at that height," Jodie practically screams.

"What's everyone talking about?" It's Amanda. Whoa. Where'd she come from? She appeared as suddenly as . . . well, as the Wicked Witch of the West.

"Oh, hello, Amanda, dear," H.H. says. Man, she really is trying to be nicer. She must have gone to meditation class this morning. She's always a little gentler after she goes to meditation class. "Height. We were talking about height." Meh. Never mind.

"What about it?" Amanda asks, slithering into the doorway.

"Just that it's a thing," I say, eager to switch topics. Remind Amanda that when she was hired she was four feet, eight inches and she's now approaching four feet, eleven inches, and she'll blow a gasket. Starting off the week with an Amanda-sized temper tantrum is no one's idea of a good time.

"What brings you here?" Jodie Howard asks. "We never get visits from you."

"Oh, nothing," Amanda says. "I got to the theatre early today, because I had a secret interview for a magazine I can't name, so I got dressed early, and here I am."

Huh. That's odd. If Amanda is anything, she's a creature of habit. In the door at fifteen minutes to Half Hour, makeup, vocal warm-up, then Jeremiah puts on her wig. She doesn't change her routine for any reason. Something's brewing. Something's fishy. Something's making my stomach flip.

"Aren't we lucky," H.H. says.

"What are those?" Amanda asks, pointing to the eyelashes in Jayne's hand.

"Her pet spiders," Jodie Howard says dryly.

"Haha, very funny, lemme see," Amanda says, sticking her arm out to grab them from Jayne, who pulls away.

"No," Jayne says. "They're mine."

"Look at *you*, you actually know how to speak," Amanda says.

"There's no reason to be mean, Amanda," I say.

"No one asked you, *Lulu*," Amanda says.

"Amanda, dear, while I know you tend to operate under the assumption that you can do or say anything you'd like, I'm here to tell you that in this dressing room, that rule does not apply," H.H. says.

"I concur. Vehemently," Jodie Howard nods. "As we used to say in the sixties, 'let's keep the peace.'"

"My *apologies*, Heather. My *apologies*, Jodie. I meant no harm." Oh, puh-lease.

Amanda glances over at Jayne, who's holding on to her boxed eyelashes like she's protecting them from a predator. "Eyelashes, hmm. Interesting," Amanda says.

"What's so interesting about it?" Jayne asks.

"It just seems . . . oh, what's the word? *Unnecessary*," Amanda says. "You won't ever need them, Jayne, because you'll never go on for *my* role. I wish you had saved your money. Bought a good book, or something. Something to keep you occupied backstage. Though I see those aren't the most expensive brand, so the book would need to be from the bargain bin—"

"That's about enough of that," H.H. says. "Milly!" she yells, turning to face Amanda square on. I've heard H.H. yell exactly three times and each time has been more epic than the last, so, brace yourselves.

"You, my dear, are what we adults call a pot-stirrer. I know, because I used to be like you, in my youth. I thought I could say or do whatever I wanted because I was talented and pretty, but the truth is the only thing

I had over everyone else was luck. Plain and simple. Sure, I was talented. I still am. And I'll admit, you're talented. But there are a lot of talented people in our city, not to mention our great big world. You didn't get this job because you're the best; you got it because you got lucky. Preparation met opportunity and some luck rained down on the two of them. Once your luck runs out, you will wish you had been nicer to people. Because all the people in this building? We have ears, eyes, and *big* mouths. And we're not afraid to tell each and every member of our beloved Great White Way just how cruel you are. There's a lot of talent out there. There's absolutely no reason to hire someone who isn't a team player."

Whoa. Someone get that on a T-shirt, ASAP.

Before the rest of us can say anything, Milly arrives, flushed from running down from the third floor. She's wiping her hands with a paper towel, which probably means she was in the bathroom. Poor gal can't even get two minutes of peace in the loo. "Everyone okay?" Her eyes jump from kid to kid, scanning for injury.

"Jodie and I have to finish getting ready," H.H. says sharply.

"Two guests was a party, but now three's a crowd," Jodie adds, with a not-so-subtle wink.

"Oh, of course. Come on, girls," Milly says, ushering us out. "Sorry to bother you, ladies."

On our way back up to the kids' floor, Amanda waits until Milly is out of earshot and whispers, "Just so we're clear, Jayne, I have no intention of letting my luck run out. You may as well give those eyelashes to Lulu. She has about as much of a chance of getting to use them as you do."

Instead of spouting off a nasty retort (because that's not her style), Jayne simply sighs and walks off. But I just can't let this go.

"Please tell me why you're so cruel to us," I say.

"Excuse me?" Amanda growls.

"I refuse to believe you're just a mean girl. There must be something else going on," I say. "You can tell me."

Amanda looks at me, her face crooked and puzzled. Like she's trying to solve a riddle or math problem. Then she settles on a solution and huffs, "I don't have to explain myself to anyone, especially you."

"All of this negativity isn't healthy," I say. "I believe what H.H. says about karma."

"And what's that?" Amanda asks.

"That it's real," I say.

"I'll believe it when I see it," she says, stomping off to the dressing room.

"If there's any justice in this world," I say under my breath, "you will."

CHAPTER
SIXTEEN

A WEEK LATER, KARMA STRIKES LIKE LIGHTNING.

"I feel sweaty," Amanda says.

It's an hour and a half before curtain, and Amanda is currently the only actor in the building. Because she's here, Milly has to get here early, too. Amanda's in the wardrobe room, having the hems on her costumes let out for the second time this month. She's—what's the expression?—growing like a weed.

"It is a bit warm in here," Bet says. "Heat kicked in when the temperature dropped last night."

"No, it's not that," Amanda says. There's no sass in her reply. I repeat: there is no sass in her reply.

"What do you mean?" Milly asks, calm but concerned. (P.S. If Amanda's mom were here, she'd be *flipping* out. Calling a private physician and making sure an ambulance is on hand flipping out.)

"I . . . I . . . I'm going to be sick." Amanda covers her mouth, Bet covers Amanda's costume, and Milly runs for a wastebasket. My mother pulls me away. I guess she's worried I'll get stomped on. Or worse.

Then worse happens.

Don't make me say it.

Okay fine. Puke. *Puke* happens. Puke *happens*.

Milly and Bet manage to get Amanda to the closest bathroom; there's no way she's going up four flights of stairs to her own bathroom in this condition. My mother drags me along to make sure Amanda's okay—I guess there's no squelching maternal instinct—so I'm sitting in the basement bathroom, listening to my archnemesis get sicker than anyone ever deserves to. I mean, it's bad. This isn't the fault of gluten or a sniffling sibling, this is worse. Much worse.

"Food poisoning," Bet says.

"I"—*PUKE*—"don't"—*PUKE*—"get"—*PUKE*—"food poisoning," Amanda pukes out.

"I grew up in a tenement in Little Italy," Bet says. "I know food poisoning when I see it." And hear it. And worse. Smell . . . ugh, gross.

"Lulu, go get Pete," Milly instructs.

"No!" Amanda gurgles.

"Amanda. The curtain goes up in an hour and twenty minutes. We need to be prepared. Just in case." Milly knows better than to tell Amanda she's not getting anywhere near that stage, let alone the upper level of the theatre. It'll be Pete's job to tell Amanda that she's got to leave through the basement exit, to make sure she doesn't get anyone else sick, in case it isn't food poisoning after all. He's the only one she'll listen to.

I scurry down the hall to the stage manager's office faster than you can say "*Les Misérables* is long but worth it" to find Pete, Susie, and Ricardo at their computers, typing away.

"You guys," I cough out. (I ran really fast, even for a mouse.) "Amanda—"

"What'd she do this time?" Susie is sooooo over Amanda and her antics. Susie is one of, like, a dozen siblings and is a former Rockette. She doesn't have patience for people who can't be team players.

"She's sick," I say. "Super sick."

"I thought her private physician promised that would never happen," Ricardo scoffs.

"Bet thinks it's food poisoning," I say. "One second, Amanda was standing in wardrobe for alterations, the next, she was puking all over the place."

"Not on the costumes? Please, tell me she didn't puke on the costumes," Pete says.

"No, Bet covered them," I say.

"Good. Sorry. Didn't mean to sound insensitive, but her costumes cost more than my first apartment," Pete says. "Okay. I'll call Jayne's mom to tell them to be here as soon as possible."

"Great," I say. "Can I help in any way?"

"Pray to the theatre gods that we've rehearsed her enough," Pete says, and he's out the door.

Praying to the theatre gods. *That* I can do.

CHAPTER
SEVENTEEN

Y OU'RE *KIDDING*," H.H. SAYS WITH THE SMILE
of a loveable Disney villain. "Food poisoning?"

"Yep," I say. "Can you believe it?"

"I can, actually. Yes, I can. To say she jinxed herself is the understatement of the year," H.H. declares, lining her lips with Rockin' Red.

"I despise throwing up. Hate it more than anything in the world. Hate. It." Jodie cringes. "Where and what did she eat? It wasn't at the deli on Forty-Third, was it? Was it the egg salad? No, don't. Don't tell me. I don't want to know. I can't live without that egg salad."

"Apparently," I say, almost happily (theatre gods and

all others, please forgive me), "it was her mom's home-made salmon."

"No! Oh, that's too rich. Mrs. My Child Only Eats Organic gives her daughter food poisoning. The *irony* is too delicious," H.H. says with a laugh. "No pun intended."

"I know, it's nuts," I say, scaling backward down the leg of the counter and onto the floor. "No pun intended, either. Now if you'll excuse me, I've got to get back to Jayne."

"I'm sure she'll be stupendous," Jodie yells. "You tell her Jodie Howard said she'll be stupendous!"

"Will do," I say. I'm pretty sure Jodie's the only person on the planet (who isn't in the circus) who can get away with saying the word "stupendous."

"And she'll get to use the eyelashes I gave her! Glad you'll be there to help her with them," H.H. says.

"Me too!" I say, hurrying out the door and up the stairs.

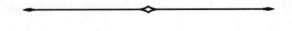

"I can't believe this is happening," Jayne says. "I'm not ready. Lulu, I'm not ready."

"Of course you are," I say, because I'm 92 percent certain she is, and 92 percent is an A, so that's good enough for me. "You hold the lash, I'll squirt on the glue."

"You can do that?" she asks.

"I've been doing it for years," I say, picking up the tube, which I'm guessing is the same size as I was at birth. I squeeze the tube and delicately apply the glue to the lash's edge. "Lightly tap the lash on your hand to take off the excess glue."

"Right," she says, doing as I instructed.

"Now apply it to your lash line, outside in," I say.

"What do you mean? Can you help?" she asks.

"Sure," I say. I climb up her arm and onto her shoulder, holding the lash like humans hold open a book, only backward and upside down. Then I line it up to her lash line, gently securing it. "There. Perfect."

"It feels funny. Like there's a bug on my eye," she says, blinking.

"Would you rather not wear them?" Milly appears with a tub of Clorox wipes to begin the Amanda-is-sick decontamination process. "I don't want them to distract you."

"No, I'm fine," Jayne says. "If Amanda wears them, I should, too."

"Blush is next," I say. "Peony Pink will look nice on you." She makes a fish face, and swipes the blush onto the apples of her cheeks. "Lovely. You're a natural."

"I've seen my sister do it," Jayne says. "She's in high school."

"Will your family be here tonight?" I ask.

"I hope so. It's so last minute, they may not all make it in in time. My grandma lives in Brooklyn, so she'll be here. And my mom drove me in, so she'll be here, too. She's over at Sardi's having a glass of wine and trying to relax."

"Fifteen Minutes. This is your Fifteen-Minute call. Fifteen Minutes, please," Pete's voice booms. "And just a reminder, company, Jayne will be on for Amanda tonight."

"Well, now it's official!" I say. The truth is, it was official the moment Pete posted it on the call-board at Half Hour. He had summoned Amanda's mom back to the theatre and explained that while *technically* he couldn't keep Amanda—or any actor—from performing, it was accepted practice across the theatre community that a stage manager's *suggestion* that a sick performer call out for the performance was as good as a command. Amanda's leaving was for the benefit of the whole company. They couldn't risk a stomach flu outbreak.

Please note: the following exchange took place in the basement bathroom.

"But it's not stomach flu; it's food poisoning," Amanda's mom had argued.

"We don't know that for sure," Pete had said.

"We do know that, because Amanda doesn't get the stomach flu. It's *food poisoning*."

"When she was sick a few months ago, it was a stomach flu," Pete had said.

"That was *not* a stomach flu; it was a side effect of her *severe* gluten intolerance and some new vitamins she was taking." (Amanda must get her knack for making things up from her mother.)

"Regardless of the cause, the fact that she's vomiting means she can spread germs," Pete had said. "And she's not getting any better."

"I'm"—*PUKE*—"fine"—*PUKE*—"really." Amanda had been huddled next to the toilet, bundled up in a sweatshirt *and* fleece, shivering.

"Our doctor is on his way with an anti-nausea pill he says will make her good as new," Amanda's mom had said, frantically checking her text messages. "I knew we should have had them on hand. He said they were too strong for him to prescribe. What a moron."

"Doctor knows best. She'll be good as new for tomorrow," Pete had reasoned. "One show won't make a difference."

"Yes"—*PUKE*—"it"—*PUKE*—"will."

"It won't," Pete had said. "I promise. It'll be your role whether you come back tomorrow or in a week."

"A *week*?!" Amanda's mom had shrieked.

"Tomorrow. We'll go one performance at a time. I have to call Half Hour, Amanda."

PUKE. PUKE.

"Okay," Amanda had said quietly. *PUUUUUKE.*

And with that, Pete had posted the change on the call-board, officially told Jayne and Milly (and me—I was there), and Amanda's mom dragged Amanda through Shubert Alley into the Marriott Marquis hotel, where she, I assume, continued to puke.

Back to the present (aka fifteen minutes until Jayne's Broadway debut!): Milly and I are going over Jayne's quick changes.

"So, after the first scene, you exit stage right, and we'll be there. We go downstairs, meet Jeremiah in the hair room, he puts the pigtails wig on you, we cross under the stage, then we head up to your dressing room for your costume change," I say.

"Remember," Milly says, "don't get flustered. Your dressers and hair people have done this over three hundred times, so just let them do all the work. It'll feel like not enough time, but it's really more than enough."

"Okay," Jayne says.

Despite the instruction, Jayne's flustered. She's staring into the dressing room mirror, running a ChapStick repetitively over her lips.

"Can I help you in any way?" Milly asks.

"No. I . . . I . . ."

"How's our girl?" Susie pops her head into the dressing room. "Feeling good?" I look to her and subtly shake my head. She makes her way into the room and squats down next to Jayne. "Can I tell you a story, Jayne?"

"Sure," Jayne says, robotically capping the ChapStick.

"When I was only a little older than you are now, I competed in a worldwide baton-twirling competition." We all give her a look. You know the look. The kind of look you give someone when they tell you they competed in a worldwide baton-twirling competition.

"Random, I know, but the point is: I was good. Really good. Ranked in the top ten girls in the world." Okay. That is *très* impressive. "But the night of the competition, I started doubting myself. My mom had me take deep breaths and reminded me that there was a reason I was there. Because I was great. Better than great. One of the best. And you, Jayne? You're one of the best."

Jayne smiles, the zombie spell breaking. "Thanks, Susie."

"So, take a deep breath and remember that you know what you're doing," Susie says. "The most important thing is to have fun. You have fun and the audience will have fun. Got it?"

"Got it," Jayne says.

"Good. See you down there," Susie says. "Milly and Lulu will make sure you keep breathing, yes?"

Before we can agree, there's a knock at the door, followed by a familiar voice I've never heard up on the kids' floor.

"Knock, knock." Holy cannoli, it's Stella. She's wearing her signature silk kimono and the classiest old Hollywood slippers you've ever seen.

"I just wanted to stop by to say break a leg, Jayne," Stella says.

"Oh. I . . . I . . . thank you," Jayne manages.

"I'll be right there with you, if you need me. We all will. Though I'm sure you'll be even more prepared than we are," Stella says.

"Oh, I . . . no." Jayne says, slowly shaking her head like she's a kid at Disney World and Snow White has just told her that she and all of the other princesses have come to the unanimous decision that Jayne is actually the fairest of them all.

"I'm never wrong," Stella says. "See you out there."

"I'll walk you downstairs," Susie says.

One random life lesson from a former world champion baton-twirling Rockette, one "break a leg" from a two-time Tony-winning Broadway legend, and they're off.

"Wow," I say. "Just . . . wow."

"Tony winner Stella James just told you to break a leg, Jayne!" Milly says. "I hope you're taking this all in."

"Yeah." Jayne nods. "It's incredible."

But I can tell her mind is elsewhere.

"What's wrong?" I ask.

"Is *she* here?" Jayne asks.

"Who?" Milly asks.

"Amanda," Jayne says, taking deep breaths, as instructed.

"No," I say. "She's over in her hotel room puking."

"This is your performance, Jayne. Your name is

posted in the lobby and since they didn't have enough time to put *At this Performance* inserts in the programs, Pete's going to make an announcement to the audience at the top of the show."

"I'm not worried about her taking the performance back. I'm worried about her showing up to watch."

"You didn't see how sick and sweaty and shivery she was," I say, hopping into Jayne's lap. "She was practically green. She's probably asleep next to the toilet or something." That's what humans do when they puke a lot, right?

"Don't worry about her," Milly says. "Just focus, breathe, and have fun."

"Will do," Jayne says. But by the way her lap is shaking, I'm not so sure she means it.

"Wardrobe delivery," Bet says. She's carrying Jayne's sparkly blue Act Two dress and vanilla velvet top-of-show dress. My mother is in her pocket, needle and thread in hand, in case of any last-minute costume emergencies.

"Come on in," Milly says.

"These are ready to go," Bet says. "Your second change is here on the rack, and the rest of your outfits are preset in the quick-change booth onstage left."

"Jeremiah says he'll put your mic up in your wig," my mom says. "But why don't you wear a mic band around your waist, too, just in case."

"Why wear the mic band around her waist if her mic is up in her wig?" I ask. I've been making a real effort lately to disagree less with my mother, but this just seems silly and I need to know her reasoning.

"Better safe than sorry," my mom says. What is it with moms and "better safe than sorry"? Do they have a yearly quota they have to hit?

"I agree," Bet says. "Let's get you dressed, Jayne."

"Okay," Jayne says.

Bet takes Jayne's vanilla velvet opening number costume off its hanger, unzips, and opens it out in front of Jayne so she can step right in.

"There," Bet says, zipping up the dress with careful ease. "Fits like a glove."

"Comfortable?" my mom asks.

"Yes," Jayne says.

"That's what we like to hear," Bet says. "See you back here for your first change."

"Break a leg, sweetheart," my mom says. Then she looks at me and winks. I know she can tell I'm wishing it were me.

But I want her to know that I'm okay, so I say, "Jayne's going to be fabulous, Mom. Just wait until you see her."

"I have no doubt," my mom says. Then she winks again. She must have something in her eye.

CHAPTER
EIGHTEEN

J AYNE!" AGNES AND HARPER HURRY OVER. "WE'RE
so excited for you!" Agnes is a member of our ensemble but she also understudies H.H., and Harper was an understudy in her first two Broadway shows, so they totally get it.

"Thanks," Jayne says. "I'm really nervous."

"Don't be," Harper says. "You'll be fantastic."

"You were incredible at your first understudy rehearsal," Agnes adds. Which is true, she was. But her performance needs to be more than her sheer talent. She needs to remember her lines and her choreography . . . her props and blocking. . . . She needs to make sure she stands downstage of the curtain in scene four or else we'll have an unconscious actress on our hands.

Most of the time, before an understudy performs in front of an audience, we have a "put-in," which is essentially a practice run that's as close as possible to the real thing. The understudy is in full costumes, sets and prop pieces are used, and the full cast participates (though they're wearing rehearsal clothes and not costumes—visualize that, it's an odd sight). We run through the show from top to bottom. It's an audience-free way for an understudy to perform the show all the way through, instead of just scenes and dance numbers here and there like we do during regular understudy rehearsal.

But there was no time for a put-in for Jayne since she only recently joined the company, so the rehearsal she's had so far, plus help from me and Milly, will have to do. We know the show, and we'll get her through it.

Places have been called and we're all standing onstage, waiting to start the overture dance. Then we hear Pete's announcement to the audience:

"Ladies and gentlemen, please take a moment to turn off all cell phones and unwrap any candies. At this performance, the role usually played by Amanda Rose Green will be played by Jayne Griffin. Thank you, and enjoy the show." We all silently jump up and down, then cheer audibly the moment the orchestra strikes up.

"Holy cow, I can't believe this, I can't . . . ," Jayne says quietly.

"Believe it," Milly says. "It's your Broadway debut."

Jayne's Broadway debut.

Not mine.

I . . .

Huh. I thought I would feel differently, but believe it or not, I'm okay with it. I'm so excited for my friend, so thankful to be a part of this show, to play the role I play backstage.

It suddenly hits me that I might never make my Broadway debut. And that's okay. What I've got and who I am is more than enough.

I'm a backstage cheerleader. A coach. A friend. I will always be a starring player in Jayne's Broadway debut story, and perhaps that's enough.

"Let's do this," I say.

We begin our overture dance, and it hasn't been this fun since the two times Maya went on. If there's one thing (most) show people know how to do, it's how to be supportive and excited for a castmate. Sure, people get envious and jealous, as we know, but for the most part, these people want to make this moment as wonderful as possible for Jayne.

We do our high kicks, our shimmies, our mouse hop, and then it's over and it's time for the show to begin. Milly and I walk Jayne to her entrance spot upstage.

"Okay," Milly says, "this is where we leave you. See you after the first scene. We'll be in the wings offstage right."

Jayne's shaking like a leaf that knows a hurricane's coming. "Can't Lulu stay?"

Wait a minute.

"You'll be okay," Milly says. "I promise."

That wasn't *exactly* a no.

"I need Lulu. It's been the two of us this whole time. She knows the blocking better than I do. Please, Milly."

Forget what I said on the previous page about being okay with—

"She can't go onstage with you, honey, I'm sorry. That would be breaking so many rules. I could lose my job."

Ugh. Never mind.

Wait. *Wait!* Holy cannoli, holy pizza pie, holy—

"Your mic is up in your wig!" I loudly whisper.

"Yes," Jayne says. "Is that bad? Should we move it to my waist? I kept the empty mic band on like your mom said I should."

Oh my goodness, my meddling mother just made this the best day of my life.

"I can sit in your mic band! Where the mic would be!"

"Yes!" Jayne says. Her shaking instantly stops. "Between the two of us, we'll get through the show with no trouble at all."

"I don't think this is a good idea," Milly says, worry in her eyes.

"I won't move, Milly, I promise. Unless Jayne needs me. One tug for 'you're doing the right thing,' two tugs for 'you're not,' okay?"

"Got it," Jayne says.

"I don't know . . . ," Milly says, absentmindedly picking at her fingernails like grown-ups do when they're nervous.

We've got literally forty-three seconds until Jayne makes her entrance, so it's now or never.

"Please, Milly. If I need help, she'll be right there. She'll keep me from making a mistake," Jayne says.

"Oh, all right. But don't tell anyone." Milly sighs. "And, Lulu. Under no circumstances are you to get out of the mic band, do you hear me?"

"Loud and clear!" I say with unmitigated glee. And as fast as you can say "The Tony goes to Audra McDonald," I'm in place in Jayne's mic band. My tail is sticking out a bit, but it's just about the same size and color as the microphone antenna, so if anyone happens to see it, they'll never know it's me. Milly zips the zipper, and I'm all locked in.

"All set?" Milly asks.

"Yep," Jayne says. I tug once. "Lulu's all set, too."

"Okay, that's your cue. Go!"

And we're through the set door and onstage.

Jayne says her first line and the audience immediately laughs. I've heard this laugh over three hundred times, but it's louder and richer than ever before because I'm not in the wings. I'm not in the dressing room. I'm not in my nest listening over the backstage monitor.

I'm onstage. The audience is right there, out in the house, *my* house, where I've spent my whole life waiting and preparing for a moment like this.

I swear to you; the air feels different out here. It's cozy and electric. Even through Jayne's costume and the mic pack pouch, I can feel the lights. They're bright and blinding just like they were when we made believe in front of H.H.'s mirror. I feel the lights shift into spotlight, and Jayne starts to sing.

JAYNE (AND I!!!) EXIT OFFSTAGE RIGHT TO FIND MILLY and 78 percent of the cast, who have been watching from the wings.

"You are a star!" Harper says.

"Honey, I couldn't have done it better myself," says Jodie.

"Thanks," Jayne says. If her head's spinning even half as fast as mine is, I'm surprised she can even form words.

"Where's Lulu?" H.H. asks. "I thought she'd be with you for the whole show."

"She decided to watch from the back of the house,"

Milly says quickly. "Time to get this girl to her next change!"

We head down to the hair room, and Jeremiah removes Jayne's banana curl wig, replacing it with wig number two: pigtails.

"Feeling okay with the mic up there?" Jeremiah says. I yank once on Jayne's dress.

"Yep!" she says. "Super comfortable."

"You sure? We've got time to move it to your waist band if you like."

"*No!*" Milly and Jayne say in unison. Jeremiah narrows his eyes with an *okay, crazies* glare.

"I mean," Jayne says, calmly, "why change things now?"

"Gotcha," Jeremiah says. "Makes sense." And I feel Jayne breathe a sigh of relief. She's certainly a well-trained singer; she totally breathes low and into her belly, even when she's not singing.

Then we hurry under the stage, passing the male

ensemble dressing room and their cheers, and back upstairs to "our" dressing room, where Bet and my mom are waiting.

"You have an exquisite voice, Jayne," Bet says. "Now. Shoes off, then dress."

"Okay . . . ," Jayne says hesitantly. I give her costume a quick tug to say, "We're good," and then Jayne perks up and says, "Okay!"

"Okay, then," Bet says, unzipping the dress. I curl my tail in as close as I can to my body, but with my tail's permanent deformity, that's easier said than done and—

"I thought Jeremiah put your mic up in your wig," Bet says.

"He did," Milly says.

"Then what is this sticking out . . . ? Lulu?"

"Hi, Bet," I say, peeking my head out of the mic pack pouch. "Hi, Mom."

"Lucy Louise." She's only pretend-reprimanding. I know my mother. She's making it seem like she doesn't know a thing about any of this to save everyone's . . . well . . . tails, but on the inside, she's thrilled I put two and two together and hopped in.

"It was my idea," Jayne says, valiantly taking the blame for what was actually a grand mouse plan. "I didn't think I could do it without her."

"Good thing you kept your mic belt on, then," Mom says. "See how things work out?" God bless my mother.

"Indeed," Bet says. From the way she and my mom are eyeing each other, five bucks says Bet was in on it, too. "So? How was it?" she asks.

"It was . . ." For once, I'm the one who can't find my words.

So Jayne helps. "It was . . . *everything*," she says.

"Well, it's far from over," Milly says. "We're one short song away from your next entrance."

"Quite right," Bet says. "Ballet slippers on. Lulu, are you staying or going?"

"She's staying," Jayne says, before I can even answer.

"She's my good luck charm."

Good luck. She said it. Without even thinking, she said what we're never supposed to say.

"Oh, no," Jayne says.

"It's just a superstition," my mother says.

"Over the years, I've heard it said hundreds of times. Nothing bad has ever come from it," Bet assures her.

"Forget it happened." Milly smiles.

"Okay," Jayne says, breathing deep. "Forgotten."

"Time to zip up," Bet says. "Tuck that tail in, Lulu, so I don't zip you, too."

"Just one sec," I say. "Mom?"

"Yes, sweetheart?"

"Thanks."

"For what, my love?" Mom says with a wink.

"For . . . everything," I say.

I duck down into the mic pack pouch, Bet zips the zipper, and we head back downstairs, passing Rosa at the stage door.

"Looking good, kiddo," Rosa says. "I've seen a lot of Broadway debuts, but this one's special."

I give Jayne's costume a tug. "You're telling me," she says.

We head through the (almost) soundproof door that separates the stage door hallway and the stage, into the wings offstage left.

"All right," Milly says. "You know your cue?"

"Yep," Jayne says. *Tug.* "And so does Lulu."

"Shhh. That's between us, all right? It's bad enough Bet and Lulu's mom know," Milly says.

"Got it," whispers Jayne, as we hear H.H. (in character) say, "Where are you, darling? Our guest is almost here!"

"That's my cue!" Jayne says, twirling out of the wings and onto the stage. Luckily, it's only five chaînés, and oh geez, this must be what sea sickness feels like. Try to spot, Lulu, try to spot.

On the final turn, I catch a glimpse of what looks

like—no, it can't be. It can't be.

But it is. I'm sure of it. Out at the back of the house, illuminated by the red exit sign, stands Amanda. Arms crossed. Hoodie on her head. Just. Watching.

Jayne puts her hand on me, and I know she's seen her, too.

In character, H.H. says, "You certainly know how to make an entrance," which is Jayne's cue to speak and Jayne says . . .

Nothing.

Never say "good luck" in a theatre. Maybe it's not a silly superstition after all.

CHAPTER
NINETEEN

H. says the line again, with a different intonation so the audience (hopefully) won't catch on. I tug twice on Jayne's dress. Nothing. I whisper the line. Nothing. Either Jayne can't hear me, or she's lost the ability to speak. *Tug. Tug.* Nothing.

No, not nothing, shaking. That stage fright from her first day has returned with a vengeance.

H.H. begins to expertly improvise a solo scene in which she fluffs the couch pillows and dusts the furniture.

With my supersonic mouse hearing, I clock Pete in the wings, whispering into his headset to the rest of the crew, *"One more minute and I take down the curtain and we say she got sick or something."*

No. Absolutely not. This will not be Jayne's Broadway debut. This will not be *my* Broadway debut. A Broadway debut I had just about given up on moments before it happened.

I will not let Amanda's fast-working anti-nausea pill ruin the night we've both dreamed of our whole lives. No. Nah. Not. Gonna. Happen.

So before you can say "Please bring *Oliver!* back to Broadway with Adele as Nancy," I'm out of the mic belt and up on Jayne's shoulder. H.H.'s eyes go wide, but she plays it cool, switching from furniture maintenance to adjusting her stockings, in an effort to mesmerize the audience with her "legs for days," I guess.

I get right up in Jayne's ear and say the line. Nothing. I say it again. Nothing.

So I go off script and say what really needs to be said.

"Do not let her take your dream from you, Jayne. You are on *Broadway*. *You.* You can do this."

I feel a tear trickle down Jayne's cheek. It hits me like a drip from a leaky, saltwater faucet.

She takes a deep, determined breath.

Then . . . she says the line.

H.H. immediately snaps back into the scripted scene, and, phew, that's a relief, everything's going to be just fine and . . . oh, no . . . I'm on Jayne's shoulder. I don't think I can get back into the mic pack pouch. What am I going to—

"What a charming little mouse you have there," Stella says. She's just made her entrance, but this isn't her entrance line. This isn't even in the script. I repeat. This isn't in the script.

"A little sidekick of sorts, I suppose?" This line is in the script. But Stella's character is referring to Jayne's character's teddy bear, who she dances with in the number that's about to begin. But instead of pointing to the teddy bear, per the blocking, Stella points to me.

"Indeed, madam," Jayne says, gently taking me from

her shoulder and placing me in her palms, thankful tears in her eyes. "A sidekick and a friend."

The audience gasps. I prepare myself for a mass evacuation and screams, but, so far, they're staying put.

"Simply marvelous," Stella says.

That's the cue for the music to begin, so even though Michael has a look on his face like he's seen . . . well . . . a mouse performing on Broadway, he signals to the orchestra to start playing, and they do.

And I spend the rest of the number front and center, onstage at the Shubert Theatre, on Broadway, with three of my favorite human beings—humans who have always treated me as an equal, humans I'd do anything for, who would *clearly* do anything for me.

Once all three gals start to sing in unison, I join in, too. And while I'm sure no one can hear me—I'm not wearing a mic and, while yes, my voice is strong and powerful, it's strong and powerful for a mouse—*I'm singing on Broadway*.

And the audience isn't running. They aren't screaming with fear. They're laughing, and—based on the few faces I can see—they're loving every minute of this. Sure, they run when they see me in the lower lobby, when they see my brothers in the alley. But since I'm up onstage, they have permission to like me. To be unafraid. Onstage, I'm not scary, I'm just part of the show. Onstage, I'm just like everyone else.

Before I know it, the number is over and the curtain falls for intermission.

CHAPTER
TWENTY

I DON'T EVEN KNOW WHERE TO BEGIN," PETE SAYS. "Thirty-five years in show business, and I don't even know where to begin."

We're up in the dressing room, after being swarmed by the entire cast and crew, who were all as in awe of what happened as I was.

"That's live theatre for you!" Dan had basically screamed.

"I can't believe it; I just can't believe it!" Jodie definitely screamed.

"Well done, Lulu. A welcome surprise." That was Stella. She hadn't screamed—she's a fairly measured person who doesn't really show too much emotion—but it was her calm praise that meant the most. Had it not been for her quick thinking, I don't know what we would have done. I certainly would not have made my full-out (and incredibly unexpected) Broadway debut.

Now, though, we're facing Pete. He's an understanding guy, but this isn't a usual misstep, like getting to the theatre late or forgetting a prop; this is big. Mouse-on-Broadway big.

"It's my fault, Pete," Jayne says. "I wasn't sure I was ready, and having Lulu with me gave me confidence."

"You got through your first number without her. What changed?" he asks. Jayne, Milly, and I hang our heads. "She was with you from the top of the show?"

"In my mic belt. She only climbed up to my shoulder because I froze and forgot my line. I saw Amanda at the back of the house, and I—"

"Wait. Amanda was watching?" Pete closes his eyes and shakes his head.

"She must have snuck in the front between numbers. She wasn't there from the top of the show. It shook me," Jayne says.

"I had to help her, Pete," I say. "I just had to."

"I allowed Lulu to ride along in the mic belt," Milly admits. "But I did not authorize a shoulder stand. You promised you'd stay in the mic band, Lulu."

"I know, Milly. I'm so sorry." As fantastic as it feels to have made my Broadway debut, it feels absolutely awful to have disappointed Milly. Nothing comes without a price, I suppose.

"Thank you for the apology," she says. "Pete, I take full responsibility."

"Sorry to interrupt." It's Susie. "I was just in the lower lobby, and you'll never guess what's happening."

"Please tell me the audience isn't rioting," Pete says, only half joking.

"The opposite," she says. "They can't stop talking about 'that cute little dancing mouse.'"

Oh my goodness.

"You're kidding," Pete says.

Susie shakes her head. "I haven't seen an audience this excited since Elphaba flew."

Oh my goodness.

"Does this mean we can finish the show together?" Jayne asks with a hopeful grin.

"If the audience is happy, I'm happy," Pete says. "We'll deal with the union and the producers later. Get ready for Act Two, girls."

OH MY GOODNESS.

"You heard the man," Milly says, beaming. "Let's get ready for Act Two! Jayne, that means the sparkly blue dress. Make sure to take a bathroom trip, too."

"I'm on it!" Jayne says, heading to the door. "Be right back."

"How are you feeling?" Milly asks, placing me on the counter so we're almost face-to-face.

"Are you still upset with me?" I ask.

"You heard Pete! The audience is happy; he's happy. He's happy; I'm happy. To be honest, I would have done the same thing if I were you."

"Then I'm feeling . . . happy!" I say. "Happier than I've ever been. When I woke up this morning, it was a typical Tuesday. Little did I know it would turn out to be the best Tuesday of my life. The best *any day* of my life."

"Company, listen up, please." Pete's voice booms over the backstage monitor. "For the sake of continuity, for the rest of this performance the role usually played by Teddy the Bear will be played by Lulu the Mouse. Have a fantastic Act Two, everybody."

"Well, once he's announced it to the company, you know what that means," Milly says.

"It's official!" Jayne says, bouncing into the room.

Official. I'm officially on Broadway.

HAVE YOU EVER HAD A MOMENT WHERE YOU FELT SO happy you could burst? Where you were sure you must be dreaming and you're just hoping no one will wake you up? I'm in that moment right now. I've spent as long as I can remember dreaming of what my Broadway debut would look like and feel like, but somehow I never dreamed this. This. This perfect, extraordinary, unexpected dream. A dream that was beyond my imagination. And I've got quite the imagination.

"See you out there, Tiny," H.H. says, popping her head into our dressing room. "You too, Jayne. You're doing brilliantly, by the way. Quite the debut. Both of you."

Jodie sneaks in behind her. "I couldn't be more proud if I were both of your mothers. Though that would involve some serious scientific advancements."

Mother. My family! "Someone needs to tell my family!" I belt.

"I'm sure they heard the announcement," H.H. says. "But I'll head down there now, just in case. Don't worry,

Tiny. They wouldn't miss this for the world."

"Five Minutes. This is your Five-Minute call. Five Minutes please," Pete's voice pipes.

"Dress time, Jayne," Milly says. "Lulu? Think you should wear your chartreuse ribbon-scarf?"

"Sure!" I say. "Can someone run downstairs to my nest to get it?"

"You left it here after Sunday's show," Milly says, reaching up to a high shelf to retrieve it. "I put it up there for safekeeping." She hands it to me, and I whip it around my neck, just like H.H. taught me.

"Excellent technique, Tiny," H.H. says, nodding approvingly.

"This is all *bashert* is what this is," Jodie Howard declares.

"Bashert?" Jayne asks.

Another Yiddish term. But I've heard Jodie say it before, so I know.

"It means, 'meant to be,'" I say, "in Yiddish."

"Bashert," Jayne says. "I like it."

"Tiny, my dear," H.H. says, patting me on the head. "To say I'm happy for you is the understatement of the year."

"You and me both," I say. "Also, I love it when you rhyme unintentionally."

"Tiny," she says, tears immediately filling her eyes, "you are very special."

"You can say that again," Jodie says. "Lulu the Broadway Mouse. Also knows Yiddish. From here on out, anything's possible."

The ladies leave, and Jayne steps into her sparkly blue dress. It fits like a glove. She looks like a little princess.

"Wow," Jayne says. "I just . . . wow."

"You look beautiful," I say.

"You do," Milly says. "And you, Miss Lulu. How about a little mascara on your whiskers?"

"Sure!" I exclaim with glee. But before Milly can pull the mascara wand out of its tube, we're interrupted.

"Milly," Rosa says over the intercom, "Amanda is on her way up. I tried to stop her, but I can't leave my post at the stage door."

"I thought she wasn't allowed backstage tonight!" Jayne says, panicked.

"You two stay here; I'll handle this," Milly says, heading out the door. "If she gets me sick, so help me . . ."

"Don't worry," I say to Jayne. "Milly will take care of it. And Pete is not going to be happy. Just get used to how your dress feels. Make sure you're comfortable twirling and sitting."

Man, I wish I had a sparkly blue dress. Maybe by next week? My mom has never made any costumes for me before because she thought it would be "out of line," but now that I'm a bona fide performer, I bet she'd be willing to sew one up in no time. No. Stop, Lulu. Be thankful for what you have. Your chartreuse ribbon-scarf is fabulous. It's Stella-approved! Focus on the present. Focus on the—

"I *need* to speak to them!" I hear Amanda say. And

before you can say "*Into the Woods*," Amanda flings open our door and we're face-to-face with the girl who almost ruined Jayne's Broadway debut, simultaneously facilitating mine. She looks smaller than she usually does—probably because she's been puking for the last three hours—but she also looks less harsh. Her arms aren't crossed; they're at her sides, just hanging there like spaghetti. She's got no makeup on, so she actually looks her age. She looks . . . gentler.

"I'm not staying. I don't want to get anyone sick. I just needed to say"—*Is that a tear?*—"you both are doing a terrific job. Jayne, I'm thankful you were so ready with such little rehearsal. You're really talented. And, Lulu. I know this is something you've always wanted, and I'm glad it's finally happening."

What is going on? Did Amanda just say something nice? Something . . . from the heart? Something generous and selfless and kind? If I somehow fell into an alternate universe, I'm happy to stay here forever.

"Thanks," Jayne says. "That means a lot."

"Yeah, thank you," I say. "How are you feeling?"

I'm prepared for Amanda to snap back like she usually does after something nice sneaks out of her, but instead she says, "A little better. But I'm exhausted. I'm going to go back to my hotel. I couldn't sleep without knowing everything was going smoothly, you know?"

"I get it," Jayne says.

"That's why," Amanda says softly.

"That's why what?" I ask.

"That's why . . . why I am the way I am," she says. "Why I can be controlling and competitive and . . . mean. I know I can be mean. I'm sorry. It's just . . . I care. I love it. I love it more than anything."

Somehow, that never occurred to me. She loves it, too. As much as I do, as much as Jayne does, as much as Maya did. As much as we wished and worked for it to happen, she wished and worked to keep it from going away. All this time, we were more alike than different.

And honestly, I'm upset with myself for not realizing it sooner.

"I'll walk you back down to your mom," Milly says.

"Sleep well," I say. "We'll see you tomorrow."

"Maybe we can all go to Westway for matzo ball soup? It's the only thing I can even think about eating," Amanda says.

"I'd like that," Jayne says. "But Lulu . . ."

"Sorry, I always forget you're not allowed off the block. We'll get delivery," Amanda says. "So no one's left out."

"That's a nice idea, Amanda," Milly says. "Let's head back down to your mom, okay?"

"Okay. Goodnight, girls. Have a great Act Two," Amanda says. "And enjoy your first Broadway Bows." It's the most genuine thing I've ever heard her say.

Until she says, "I don't want to end up like Darcy Monroe." *That's* the most genuine thing I've ever heard her say. And it explains so much.

"You won't," Jayne says.

"Not a chance," I add.

She smiles at us, her tired eyes filling with apology. And a tacit promise to try to change.

She and Milly head out and wind their way back downstairs.

"Did that really just happen?" Jayne asks.

"It did," I say. "Wow."

"Maybe we'll all be friends now," Jayne says, touching up her lipstick. "I'd like it better that way."

"Me too," I say. And I suddenly feel a huge pang of guilt. And gratitude. All this time, it's been all of us against Amanda. And now, because of Amanda, we were both able to make our Broadway debuts. Life's funny like that, I guess. The puzzle pieces of our lives don't make sense until they're all put together. Amanda was a puzzle piece I couldn't find a place for. A piece I was bothered by. A piece I wished I could get rid of. And now she'll forever be the piece my puzzle wouldn't be complete without.

I'll tell you one thing. Tomorrow, over matzo ball soup and saltines, I will apologize to Amanda for not trying harder to understand her. For making her a scary "other" just like most humans do to mice. Yes, she was mean, but we were all mean sometimes, in our own ways. Sure, Amanda was a bully to me and Maya and Jayne, but we were bullies, too; it was us against her. We talked about her behind her back. I made fun of how much blush she wears. There was a part of me that was even happy when she got sick!

Jodie is right. This is all bashert. All of this happened for a reason. Amanda was meant to learn that it's okay to be vulnerable. That it's okay to admit you're scared or jealous or that sometimes, when you love something so desperately, it makes you act out, because it's your instinct to protect the thing you love. And that it's better to apologize for your actions rather than becoming defensive and combative.

And I was meant to learn that I must, must, must

see the good in others. I must try to understand them, instead of putting them in a box marked, "Don't bother: too difficult." I must be brave enough to ask, "What's wrong?" over and over until the person (or mouse) is ready to give an answer. More than anything, I must never make anyone the enemy. I must always choose faith over fear. Love instead of hate. I'm excited for the sun to rise and for it to be a new day. A fresh start for the ladies in the third-floor dressing room.

"Places, please, this is your Places call for Act Two; Places, please."

Holy cannoli, I got so caught up in my plans to become a better mouse I almost forgot I have a show to do!

"We'd better go," Jayne says.

I don't hop into her mic belt. I stay out in the open, up on Jayne's shoulder, because I can.

I'm ready to be the best Teddy Bear understudy Forty-Fourth Street's ever seen.

CHAPTER
TWENTY-ONE

I T'S OVER IN THE BLINK OF AN EYE. I'VE HEARD actors say that my whole life, and I'd always thought they were exaggerating. But after six scenes, five musical numbers, four costume changes for Jayne—including out of the sparkly blue dress and back into it for the finale—we're at Bows, and all I can say is I'm glad I had intermission to take a breath and absorb what was happening. Because Act Two is over in the blink of an eye.

Jayne has the second-to-last bow, so we've got about sixty seconds to wait.

"Let's rehearse," Jayne says. She puts me in her palm, holds her hand out, then curtsies.

"I don't want you to feel like you can't take a full-out bow," I say. I'd define a full-out bow as what Stella does. She strides out, head held high, takes in the audience, then folds in half at her waist, almost touching her hands to the ground. "One of the many reasons she's an icon," Chris whispered to me after our first preview as we watched Bows from the wings. "No one bows like Stella James."

"Amanda curtsies, so I'll curtsy," Jayne says. "It's the choreography."

"Okay, girls, it's time," Milly says.

"Here we go," Jayne says. "It's been an honor, Lulu."

"Right back at ya, my friend," I say, fighting the urge to cry.

Jayne runs onto the stage, me in her hands, and the audience leaps to its feet. Jayne's mom and dad and grandma and siblings start the standing ovation. Jayne's dad cheers, looking to Jayne's mom, who wipes away tears, first from her husband's cheek, then from hers.

Our cast is hooting and hollering; Jayne is crying. She curtsies once, then puts her hand out like we rehearsed, showing me off. The audience cheers. I take a curtsy of my own. We join the rest of the company and all extend our arms out, pointing to Stella, who strides out as confidently as ever and takes a few epic bows. Then she takes Jayne by the hand—she did this with Maya, too— and leads her center stage.

"Take another bow, Jayne," Stella says. "You too, Lulu."

We do as we're told, and the audience cheers again, and then we all form a line to bow as a company. The choreography calls for linking hands, so Jayne looks to Stella, unsure of what to do with me. My beloved H.H. saves the day, plopping me in her pocket, which, luckily, is fairly see-through.

"Can't have you getting hurt, Tiny," she says.

So we take one last bow, and though I wish I could be out in the open with them, I'm actually happy to have a moment by myself in H.H.'s pocket. I can make out the hazy silhouette of the audience. I can hear their applause. I can feel the lights. But I'm also able to close my eyes and take a moment to realize what I've just done.

I made my Broadway debut.

Me.

Lucy Louise.

Lulu.

The Mouse.

THE CURTAIN COMES DOWN, AND I'M OUT OF H.H.'S pocket faster than you can say "Did you hear the news? There's a mouse on Broadway!" The company swarms me and Jayne, a customary sight when an understudy goes on, but it feels extra special tonight.

"Start popping the champagne," Jodie shouts. "History was made today!" Everybody cheers and shouts (but they don't whistle, obviously), and then I see them.

My family. Walt, Matty, Timmy, Benji, my mom, and my dad. H.H. sees them, too, so she lets me down and we scurry toward one another in leaps so wide I'd suspect Susie would deem them *grands jetés*. (That's "big leaps" in French.)

"Lulu. You're on Broadway," my dad says quietly, almost like he can't believe it. And that's it. That does it. Now I'm crying. I'm crying harder than I think I ever have. Because I've never been this happy. Because I've never seen my parents so happy. Because I could never have done this without them. *Them*. All of them. My theatre family and my Mouse family.

My mom hugs me so tight, it's almost impossible for my dad and brothers to join, but they manage to squeeze in. (And my brothers will do just about anything to get out of a hug, so this is big deal.)

"Oh, Lucy Louise," my mom says. "It's all I've ever wanted for you."

"Nice job, Lu," Matty says. "You looked good up there."

"I bet you'll get a mention in all the papers," Timmy says proudly.

"You really did it," Benji says. (He's crying, too, by the way.)

"I've got some notes," Walt says, grinning. Man, he's a smart aleck, and I love him for it.

Jayne hurries over, her sparkly blue dress glistening under the lights. "Lulu's family!" she beams. "Wasn't she wonderful?"

"She was," my mom says. "And so were you, Jayne. Quite the debut."

"I literally couldn't have done it without Lulu," she says. "Guess what? They got us a cake! From some place called Amy's Bread!"

"That's the best cake in these here parts," Benji says, blushing like a . . . cowboy? First, Maya and now, Jayne. Why is my brother so awkward around girls?

"Good to know," Jayne replies with a wink. "Can't wait to try it. I'm starving. See you all downstairs in the

lower lobby? I'm just going to get out of costume. Hopefully, it's not the last time I say that!"

<hr/>

AN HOUR OR SO LATER, I TAKE A BREAK FROM THE
lower lobby party (and the delicious Amy's Bread yellow
cake with pink frosting) to sneak up to the stage. Aside
from my twenty seconds in Heather Huffman's pocket,
I haven't had a moment alone, and I feel like I need it.

The stage is clear of props and scenery; it's all been
neatly put back in its assigned spots by our hardworking
crew. The house lights are dim, and the only light onstage
is the ghost light, its lone bulb burning bright. I've never
actually been up here at this time of the night. It's so
peaceful and quiet, though the air still seems to hum with
hints of music, laughter, and applause.

I stand center stage and breathe deep. I close my
eyes and take a moment to process what just happened.
To give thanks for what just happened. It was a Tuesday

like any other, and then it wasn't. Faster than you can say "And the Tony goes to *Hamilton*," my life changed forever.

Thanks to my determination and preparedness, the love and support of my family and my theatre family, and a little bit of luck (courtesy of food poisoning and stage fright), we found a way to make something happen that had never happened before. I am officially the first mouse ever to perform on Broadway.

My moment.

My magic.

My miracle.

I may be the first, but let me be far from the last.

The End

I, *Lulu the Mouse*, hereby recommend:

IF YOU CAN VISIT NEW YORK . . .

- See a Broadway show. (Obviously.)

- When you go to a Broadway show, make sure to look up at the ceiling. Broadway theatre ceilings are magical. (If you spot a star, make a wish. It worked for me!)

- Mind your manners while you're at the theatre:

  1. Don't put your feet up on the seats or on the stage.

  2. Don't talk during the performance. (FYI, whispering counts as talking.)

  3. Don't play with or read your Playbill during the performance—the actors can actually see when you do, because the Playbills are bright white on the inside! Plus, the paper makes noise.

  4. Don't bring food or drink, other than water, into the theatre (unless you want a visit from the Hooligans).

5. If you must eat because you have blood sugar issues or something, please unwrap your candy or cough drop before the overture starts.

6. Dress nicer than you would to go to the grocery store, please. Church clothes, school-picture clothes, Grandma's-birthday-party clothes—those outfits should be perfect.

7. Turn off all electronic devices! All the way off! That way not a sound, light, or camera flash* will distract the actors and other theatregoers. You've come to the theatre for a reason. Leave your life, troubles, and worries behind for a couple of hours and escape into the world of the show.

• Visit Radio City Music Hall. Specifically, see the Rockettes perform.

*Do not, under any circumstances, photograph or take videos of the performance.

- Get food at:

  1. Amy's Bread on Ninth Avenue between Forty-Sixth and Forty-Seventh Streets for delicious treats, including but not limited to: orange butter cookies, yellow cake with pink frosting, red velvet cake with whipped cream frosting, chocolate cake with chocolate frosting, and hot chocolate.

  2. Don Giovanni's on Forty-Fourth and Ninth for pizza.

  3. Café Un Deux Trois for dinner. (They provide crayons and let you draw on the placemats!)

  4. Westway Diner for matzo ball soup.

  5. Burger Heaven (the one by Saks Fifth Avenue is the best) for a tuna sandwich on a toasted roll with lettuce and tomato, onion rings, and a black-and-white shake. (Note: this recommendation is courtesy of my BFF, Jayne.)

- Don't forget to visit Central Park! I've never been, but I hear it's something to see.
- If it's your thing, see a Mets or Yankees game. If you see a Yankees game, just don't tell my dad or Dan and Artie, unless you want to get into a whole conversation about why the Mets are better than the Yankees. The same applies to the Giants and the Jets. Though I really find football painfully boring to watch. All they do is run around for fifteen seconds, then fight, and argue, and grunt . . . Okay. I'm done.
- And if you forget toothpaste? Visit a Duane Reade! Need a ginger ale? Visit a Duane Reade! Need pretty much anything? Duane Reade!
- Don't forget, New Yorkers might seem a little mean or harsh, but we're really nice! Feel free to ask for directions; just make sure you don't block traffic or a subway door while you do it.

- And finally, do not freak out if you see a mouse (or a rat). We're more afraid of you than you are of us, promise.

  If you can't make it to New York just yet . . .

- See any theatre, anywhere: school plays, community theatre, national touring companies . . . it's all live theatre and it's all fabulous!

- Perform any theatre, anywhere: at your school, at your local community center, in your parents' basement. If you love theatre, you'll love performing it, no matter what the venue.

- Play dress-up and make believe. (News flash: that's being an actor!)

- Listen to any Bernadette Peters recordings.

- Get to know the work of Elaine Stritch (when you're old enough).

- Listen to anything composed by Stephen Sondheim.

- Watch *The Wizard of Oz*, *The Little Mermaid*, *Hocus Pocus*, *The Sound of Music*, *Annie*, and *Mary Poppins*.

- Try yoga. It's relaxing and good for your mind. And, on the off chance you (like me!) are working toward a full split, yoga will help you get there.
- Learn French, even if it's just a few words. It's such a pretty language, and it makes me feel fancy.
- Be a good friend. Be loyal. Be honest. Be kind.
- Be thankful for what you have and work for what you want.
- Stand up for what's right and what you believe in.
- Be yourself. It's the only thing that makes you different from everyone else.
- Eat cheese. The stinkier, the better.

Until next time, dear reader! With love, gratitude, and hope for us all,

Lucy Louise

aka Lulu the Broadway Mouse

Acknowledgments

F IRST, THANK YOU TO MY AGENT, FRIEND, AND fairy god-Yente, Linda Epstein, for your support, hard work, and chutzpah. If I've said it once, I've said it a hundred times: *you're the best agent ever*. To Julie Matysik, Adrienne Szpyrka, and the team at Running Press Kids, I am so thrilled to be making my authorial debut with you. Thank you for taking a chance on me. For hearting all over my manuscript, for appreciating and understanding the story I wanted to tell, and for finding ways to make it even stronger.

Thank you to my parents, who gave me life and made it a great one. For introducing me, at a *very* early age, to the wonders of musical theatre. Thank you for the childhood serenades, dances, and handmade costumes, the voice and acting lessons, the endless drives to the city and waits in audition rooms, for drying my tears when I didn't get the job, and for cheering me on when I finally did.

Like Lulu, I am the first in my family to perform on Broadway. I am the first in my family to do a lot of things, and I say this with great humility and endless gratitude to those who came before me and paved the way. The choices I've made were simply not options for them. I have been able to choose "make believe" as my profession, and I love my job with all my heart.

Thank you to my *Gypsy* family for making my Broadway debut an absolute dream. (Reader: I'm not exaggerating. It was an absolute dream.) As much as I treasure those sixteen months working together, I treasure the friendships that remain strong and true. This book is a tribute to my show biz beginnings and, in turn, a tribute to you.

A special shout-out to Heather Lee, who has, from New York to Los Angeles and back again, cared for me like I'm her own. And to Tim Federle, thank you for answering my endless questions and for being supportive of the fact that your lil' sis wants to be just like you when she grows up.

To the company of *Straight*, thank you for bringing me back home again.

To my husband, Kevin, who's just so nice to me, and who knows the answers to questions like, "Is it 'further' or 'farther'?" I love you. And I'm thankful for you every day.

Other notable mentions include but are not limited to: Lucy Gagliardi, Louise Pucciarelli, Liz Kossnar, Michael Walek, Julie Halston, Cady Huffman, Sophie Flack, Ali Peyser, Matt Smith McCormick, Kim Yau, Susan Lubner, Jessica Rinker, Rocco Staino, Frank Pugliese, Priscilla Becker, Peter Catalanotto, and the creative writing department at Columbia University.

If you had asked me twenty years ago, as a kid just

entering show business, what I would be doing at this very moment, I would never have said, "Writing the acknowledgments for my first book!" The (sometimes bumpy and traffic-riddled) yellow brick road of my life has led me here, to this very unexpected and welcome debut, and that's just dandy for this Dorothy.

Finally, to you, dear reader. I've a sneaking suspicion we share similar dreams, you and I. So, to you, I say this: "If I can do it, you can do it."

A SNEAK PEEK AT
JENNA GAVIGAN'S
NEXT BOOK

HERE'S <u>THE</u> NEWS

I HAVE SOMETHING TO TELL YOU, DEAR READER. Fair warning: I might (definitely) cry.

Our show is closing.

I just . . .

I guess I should do as Fraulein Maria advises and "start at the very beginning" so you can understand how we got here. (Once you understand how we got here, if you wouldn't mind explaining it to me, that'd be fab.)

It makes sense that the beginning of this story would pick up where the last one left off, right? (If you just answered, "Of course right!" bravo to you, tiny Yente.) So, although it is currently spring and my fellow cast members have been donning sockless shoes and jean jackets to match the warm breeze blowing through Shubert Alley, let's rewind to the depths of winter, puffy coats, snow boots, and blustery winds, aka a few days after my Broadway debut. Back to when my heart was bursting with joy, pride, exaltation . . . I could continue to list other applicable emotions, but we'd be here all day.

Okay. Here goes everything.

CHAPTER
ONE

EXTRA! EXTRA! READ ALL ABOUT IT!" TIMMY hollers. At least I think that's what he's hollering. His speech is mumbled because he and my other three hooligan brothers each have their mouths wrapped around a corner of this weekend's massive Arts section of the *Times*, and they're slowly maneuvering it into our house, like they're crew guys moving a cumbersome set piece. Speaking of crew guys, it was Dan and Artie who arrived at work this morning with easily fifty copies of the paper—enough for everyone in the building. They tried to get a copy downstairs to me, but the Hooligans intercepted it. Apparently, Benji said, "We'll take it from here, you clever gentlemen." (In other news, Benji has stopped talking like a cowboy and started talking like a fictional English butler.) Sure, it would have been easier to have a human carry the hefty newspaper downstairs, but my brothers wouldn't hear of it. If I could make it to Broadway, they could certainly handle weekend *Times* transportation.

"Put it down over here, boys, where we can all see it," my mother instructs.

The Hooligans plop the paper down, and my mom smooths it out with her tail. (Five bucks says later she'll ask Bet to iron it before asking one of the carpenters to frame it.)

"May I do the honors?" Timmy asks.

"You are our resident newspaper aficionado," I say.

Timmy clears his throat, then reads, "Shubert Theatre Makes History with Lulu the Broadway Mouse." Right below the headline is a huge photograph of me in Jayne's palm during Act Two, both of us with our left legs in a high kick. After the show, we found out that our sound guy,

Randall, who dabbles in photography, went to the back of the house during Act Two to make sure our debuts were documented. The *Times* bought a bunch of photos from him and now Randall can take that trip to Hawaii he's been dreaming about.

"Wow," Walt says. "That's some headline, Lu."

"The front page of the Arts section," my dad says. "My little girl."

"Everyone told you it wasn't possible," my mother says. "Even me. I'm so glad you didn't listen, Lucy Louise."

"Me too, Mom," I say.

Cut to Benji the Brit "not crying!" beside me.

"Keep reading, bro," Matty says.

The seven of us curl up around the newspaper, and each other, as Timmy continues to read.

On Tuesday evening, toward the end of the first act, a tiny mouse named Lulu made a surprise appearance onstage at the Shubert. By the curtain call, that tiny mouse had become a big star . . .

CHAPTER
TWO

Y OU COULDN'T BUY A BETTER HEADLINE!" Jodie
Howard proclaims. "And believe me, I've tried."
She pulls her sand-colored wig cap over her
pin-curled noggin, then turns to me and H.H., suddenly
serious as all get-out. "I'm kidding, of course. I would
never buy a headline."

"Of course you wouldn't," I say.

"This is the kind of article an actor dreams of, Tiny,"
Heather Huffman says. "Are you happy with it?"

"Of course," I say. "I mean, it's great for me, but it's
great for everyone else, too, right?"

"ABSOLUTELY!" Jodie shouts. "Free publicity is

the best publicity!" She dots concealer under her eyes and begins blending with her purple makeup sponge. "We're sold out for both shows today! You've made us a hit again, darling."

"If you had any use for money, I'd say it were time for a raise," H.H. says in that matter-of-fact way she does. "Perhaps there's something else we can negotiate for you? A weekly cheese platter delivery? A cushy new bed? A larger assortment of ribbon scarves?"

"Is it ridiculous to say being allowed to perform is payment enough?" I ask.

The looks on H.H.'s and Jodie's faces confirm that, yes, it is ridiculous, and I realize that me declaring out loud that I don't feel the need to be compensated for my hard work is basically pooh-poohing the strides made by generations of human women. If I'm going to blaze a trail for future generations of thespian mice, I'd better make it clear I know my worth.

"I'll ask for the cheese platter," I say.

"Good," H.H. says, retrieving a brand-new eyeliner—Cup O' Cappuccino—from a reusable Duane Reade tote. "Whatever the ask, if I know one thing for sure, it's that producers never get rid of their cash cow. Or their cash mouse, in this case." She lets out a fluttery laugh. "I think it's safe to say your job is secure, Tiny. Now. Are you sure you're still up for our preshow routine? I'd understand if you need to get up to the third floor and prepare for your own show."

"I will never give up our preshow routine," I say. "You're stuck with me."

"All right then," H.H. says. "My eyelash, please."

I scoot across their dressing room counter; my speed is slowed a bit by H.H.'s scratchy new bamboo place mat—aka her "much-needed touch of Zen." I knock the cover off the lash container, pick up her left lash, and stride it over to her. Just like I've done for three hundred forty-three performances, just like I'll do for many, many more.

"Not to gossip," Jodie Howard whispers loudly, "but . . .

I am surprised that with Amanda back from her sickbed she hasn't made a fuss about you being her new costar."

"I wasn't going to say anything, but now that you've said something, yes. It is incredibly surprising," H.H. replies.

"Life's surprising," I say.

"Indeed, it is," H.H. says, eyeing me suspiciously before closing her left lid to apply its lash.

Just between us, dear reader, my third-floor dressing room mates and I decided it was best not to broadcast our unanimous decision to turn over a new leaf and get along. We didn't want anyone else's opinions to influence things, you know? Believe me, it's tough for me not to divulge every detail to H.H. But Amanda's confession about why she acted the way she did, and my realization about how we all could have treated her better? We think it's best we keep those experiences between the four of us: me, Milly, Amanda, and Jayne. The hope is the rest of the company will sense our fresh start, without us having to explicitly state "We're going to get along now!" and that jolt of positivity will brighten up our backstage like a fresh coat of paint.

"In other news, I will be missing two performances next week to shoot a television pilot. Guest star. Possible *recurring*. I'm thrilled."

Bless Jodie Howard for her ability to steer the conversation back to her and away from topics that make me feel like I'm lying to my best H.H.

"Which one?" H.H. asks. "The one about the family who owns the bookstore?"

"No," Jodie says. "No, I was deemed 'too wise' for that one." She rolls her eyes and snorts some saline nasal spray. "That's show biz speak for 'too old,' Lulu."

"Got it," I say. I got it before she told me but would never have said it out loud. I mean, how could someone be "too wise" to own a bookstore? Honestly.

"The one about the Nantucket cop who solves crimes with the chef of his local seafood restaurant?" H.H. asks.

How she made it through that description without laughing, I'll never know.

"They said I 'wasn't believable' as someone who
'shucks oysters,'" Jodie says, decorating the statement
with her signature air quotes. "No, I booked *Apartment*.
Half-hour comedy. Single camera. Very *Downton Abbey*
but set on the Upper West Side in a prewar co-op." (FYI,
"booked" is show biz speak for getting the part.)

"Sounds fun," H.H. says. And, yes, I do sense a hint
of envy that she's doing her best to repress. The gal's only
human, ya know?

"Fifteen Minutes, this is your Fifteen-Minute call.
Fifteen Minutes, please," Pete's voice pipes through
the monitor.

"Congrats on your guest star, possible recurring,
Jodie!" I say. "H.H. and I will miss you next week."

"Yes, Lisa is lovely in your role—" H.H. starts.

"I hope not *too* lovely," Jodie panics.

"—but she's not you, my friend. *You* are one of a

kind. And speaking of one of a kind, Tiny, you'd better head upstairs and get ready. We'll see you at the overture dance."

"See you in fifteen!" I say. But before I go, I whisper into her ear, "You'll book a television role soon, H.H. I just know it."

She pats me on the head and says, "From your lips to Casting's ears, Tiny."

And then, faster than you can say "There's no business like show business," I'm off. Down the leg of their dressing room table, out the door to the second-floor hallway, and up the stairs to the third floor and *my* dressing room. *Our* dressing room. Amanda's, Jayne's, Milly's, and mine.

What's that you say? *Do you have your own name plaque on the door yet, Lulu?* Well, right now all I have is a piece of printer paper Milly fashioned into a name plaque. Pete did put a place for me to sign in on the call board, though! Rosa rubs a marker on my foot and then holds me up so I can use my foot as a stamp.

Once it's decided that this part is mine for good, I'm sure Pete will turn the printer paper hanging on our dressing room door into an official name plaque faster than you can say "Please come back to Broadway, Tony winner Kristin Chenoweth."

Oh yes, I forgot to mention. *Technically,* I'm still an understudy. Despite what H.H. said about the producers never getting rid of their cash cow-mouse, despite making the cover of the Arts section of the *Times,* despite five stellar performances, this role isn't technically mine until the producers say it is.

This might be a show, but it's also a business.

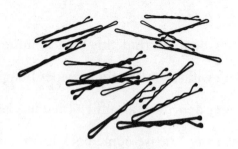

CHAPTER
THREE

L ULU, DO YOU NEED ME TO MAKE ROOM FOR YOU?"
Amanda asks. Nicely.

I'll hold so you can pick your jaw up off the floor.

"No, I'm good," I say. "But thanks for asking."

"Of course," Amanda says. "I want you to feel included."

I look at Jayne and Jayne looks at Milly and Milly just smiles with contented relief. Amanda's trying a bit too hard to be nice, but over-the-top effort is definitely better than zero effort. It's as if someone dialed her nice meter from one to one hundred and now the water's boiling over in her pot and she needs to turn the heat down just a tiny bit so we can land on a rolling bubble and sorry for the mixed metaphor.

"Thanks," I say. "Don't worry. I do."

"I was thinking with the weather as bad as it is, it might be fun to order in Chinese for in between shows," Milly says. "Thoughts?"

"Yes, please!" Jayne says.

"I'm always in the mood for those crunchy noodles that come in the little bag," I say. We mice love a crunchy food. Helps keep our teeth in good shape. The crunchier the better.

"Sure," Amanda says. "I finally have my appetite back."

"We'll look at the menu during intermission," Milly says, practically beaming from how easy that just was.

"Five Minutes, this is your Five-Minute call," Pete's voice commands. "Five Minutes, please."

"Knock, knock," Jeremiah says. "Ready for your wig, Amanda?"

"Of course," she says with a smile. "Come on in."

Jeremiah stands behind Amanda, positioning the wig directly over her head. She reaches up in front of her face, hooks her thumbs under the wig's lace—REAL HUMAN HAIR is hand tied into a lace cap of sorts to form the wig—and Jeremiah glides the wig onto her head. He puts one pin in. A second. A third. Not a peep from Amanda. Until . . .

"Thanks so much, Jeremiah," Amanda says. "I really appreciate it."

"Sure thing," Jeremiah says.

For the record, Amanda's been this nice ever since she returned to the show on Wednesday evening, but I think everyone just assumed the good vibes would wear off faster than the food poisoning did. But so far, so good.

I was, of course, a bit worried about my first performance with Amanda. My first two shows were also Jayne's first two shows, so our only experience performing our roles was with each other. But sharing the stage with Amanda is truly a delight. I doubt I would have felt the same a week ago; a week ago she probably would have twirled me into the orchestra pit. But now that we're friends, things are just fabulous.

"I'll see you after your first exit," Jeremiah says. "Have a good show, ladies."

"You too!" I say. I can't tell you how incredible it feels to know that "Have a good show" truly applies to me, too.

"By the way, Lulu," Jeremiah says, crouching down from his towering height so we're closer to eye level, "that *Times* write-up was really something. So proud of you. You too, Jayne."

"Thanks," Jayne says quickly.

"What *Times* write-up?" Amanda asks.

Jeremiah's eyes go wide and then shut as he emits a soft *guhhhhh*, like he just dropped his cell phone into a sewer grate.

"What *Times* write-up?" Amanda asks again.

"There's a little article in the paper today about Lulu's debut," Milly says. "I just assumed you saw." In truth, we weren't sure whether Amanda had seen it or not, but Milly, Jayne, and I agreed that it was probably best not to bring it up.

About the Author

JENNA GAVIGAN GREW UP DREAMING OF BROADWAY. As a teenager, she made her Broadway debut in *Gypsy* opposite Bernadette Peters. Since then, she's appeared in a handful of films, on a gaggle of television shows, and on stages east and west. A fourth generation New Yorker, Jenna graduated with a BA in creative writing from Columbia University, where she focused on fiction, television, and screenwriting. She lives in a teeny tiny Manhattan apartment with her husband, Kevin. Like Lulu, Jenna loves cheese, regularly quotes musicals, and continues to dream of Broadway. This is her first novel. Visit her online at iamjennagavigan.com and on Twitter and Instagram @Jenna_Gavigan.